STAND ALONE

Cait Wilson

Stand Alone
by Cait Wilson
Cover design by Cubist

Published by EDLINKS® Press
PO Box 205
Essex Junction, VT 05453
United States of America
edlinkspress@edlinks.com

ISBN: 978-1-967024-03-2

First Printing, 2025

The life stories in this book are a work of fiction inspired by real events and people. While certain elements are drawn from factual occurrences, the characters, some names, and specific details have been altered or fictionalized for dramatic and creative purposes. Any resemblance to actual persons, living or dead, is purely coincidental.

While the life stories are fictionalized, there are portions of this book that are based on factual information and research to the best of the author's knowledge. While every effort has been made to ensure accuracy, the author and publisher disclaim any liability for errors or omissions, and readers should consult professional advice when necessary.

*To those who may have lost their way,
here's to finding our way back.
And to the little ones just beginning,
may you stand alone from the start.*

CONTENTS

STAND ALONE

a. To not be influenced by other things or people

b. Complete by itself

c. Intended, designed, or able to function independently

INTRODUCTION

Sofia only had a few weeks left to live, and instead of reminiscing fondly on her life, she was tormented by the regret of not having done what she wanted. At just fifty years old, there was still so much she had hoped to do and accomplish, but her time had run out. Her regrets loomed over her during those final weeks like a dark cloud, reminding her life is short and we need to be intentional with the little time we have.

Throughout her life, Sofia did what was expected of her. She married her high school sweetheart and settled down in a nice home nestled within a picture-perfect suburban neighborhood. She had four children whom she loved dearly, and she and her husband were married for thirty years. On paper, she had done everything right and built a wonderful life for herself.

While her kids brought immense joy into her life, Sofia was deeply unhappy overall. Her husband was toxic and made her life miserable for decades. It was easier to appease him than stand up to his bad behavior, so day after day she brushed everything under the rug. She quietly resented him and spent most of her time dreaming of the day she could live on her own, in peace, doing what she wanted, like traveling the world.

One day, Sofia was out to lunch with her youngest daughter, Renata—"Ren" for short—who somberly turned to her and asked, "Are you happy with him?" Sofia placed her hand on her forehead, closed her eyes, and started to cry because, if she was honest, she wasn't happy at all. "Why are you still with him? He makes your life miserable," Ren questioned. Although Sofia hadn't been happy for a while, she had been willing to sacrifice her own happiness if it meant keeping the family together. Her daughter replied, "If you're not happy, you need to leave him. What's most important to us is that you're happy."

Sofia couldn't sleep that night because her daughter's words kept rattling around in her head. She'd decide to leave, then would get cold feet and talk herself through the reasons why she couldn't. Leaving felt too scary, so she decided to see if she could make her situation a bit better by standing up for herself more. But, every time she tried, her husband would get furious, making things worse. After going back and forth with her decision, she realized her best chance at happiness was to leave.

After Ren graduated from college, Sofia finally mustered up the courage to leave her husband. She packed up all of her belongings and moved into her own place. It wasn't much, but she was finally free from her husband's grasp and able to live the life she had dreamt of over the past thirty years. She immediately started making plans to go to Italy to visit her distant relatives and, after that, to Norway to see the northern lights.

However, just a few short months later, she started to feel ill. She assumed she'd recover within a week or so, but her condition was far more serious than she initially thought. Despite not showing symptoms until recently, she underwent a series of tests and was diagnosed with stage 4 cancer–it was terminal. Within a few months, she became too sick and feeble to even leave her bed, forcing her to cancel all the trips and plans she had made.

During her final weeks, instead of reflecting happily on a life well-lived, Sofia was overwhelmed with regret over all the things she never did. She sobbed in her bed, cursing herself, "I should have left a long time ago. I wasted so much time." Her heart ached, and a pit formed in her stomach as she thought about all the places she would never see, the special moments from her children's lives she would miss, the grandchildren she wouldn't get to meet, and the fact that she would never know what true love or a peaceful life felt like.

The only thing she could do was try to ensure no one else made the same mistake. Ren visited her every day, and each day, Sofia told her she needed to do what she wanted in life. Each time, Ren softly smiled and nodded in agreement that she would.

Over the weeks, Sofia's health continued to decline, and it was clear the end was near. On her final day, she looked at Ren and pleaded one last time, "Remember to do what you want in life." Fighting back tears, Ren nodded. "You don't have to worry anymore, Mom. I will." A few heart-wrenching hours later, Sofia passed away while holding her daughter's hand, and Ren hoped her mom had finally found peace.

Several months later, Ren decided to go on all of the trips her mom had planned. She went to Italy and ate pasta with their long-lost relatives and then went to Norway, where she saw the brightest display of the northern lights. In each place, she scattered some of her mom's ashes, hoping somehow, some way, her mother was experiencing it all too. At the very least, she hoped her mom was looking down on her, proud that she kept her promise of doing what she wanted in life.

Sofia's story is incredibly heartbreaking but unfortunately not unique. One of the biggest regrets people have at the end of their lives is not living on their own terms. People do what others expect instead of what they actually want, resulting in many people being haunted by regrets about everything they missed out on.

It's shockingly easy to get swept up in living the life that's expected of us. There are powerful and invisible forces that influence us to follow the crowd every day. We're programmed to try to fit in, and fitting in is so ingrained and automatic that we often don't realize we're living the life others expect of us instead of the life we truly want.

About a year later, Ren came to the painful realization that, much like her mom, she had been living the life others expected of her. As a people pleaser with nonexistent boundaries, she was willing to sacrifice herself for other people's comfort and happiness in order to belong. Her time was monopolized by obligations and expectations. She would say yes when she really wanted to say no. When she would finally muster the courage to say no, the guilt and worry over what people thought of her or if they'd be mad would eat her alive until she eventually caved. Her life didn't feel like her own; it was the byproduct of what everyone else wanted, and it was making her deeply unhappy.

Without her mother there to brighten her world, Ren felt the full weight of her unfulfilled life. Her life had become a tangled web, and the more tangled it got, the more suffocated she felt. The only viable path forward she saw was to start over. So, she moved out of state for grad school, and for the next ten years, she worked to untangle the life she had carelessly cultivated over the past several decades. She had to figure out who she was and what she truly wanted without the external influences and pressures from back home, and then she began intentionally rebuilding her life until it brought her genuine happiness. Inspired by her mom, her ultimate goal was to create a life she'd be proud of and celebrate in her final days with zero regrets.

Reclaiming her life was a difficult process, but the key was developing the courage to stand alone. She first learned about the idea of standing alone from Brené Brown in her book, *Braving the Wilderness*. To this day, it's her all-time favorite book because she found it when she was smack dab in the middle of trying to reclaim her life. The book gave Ren the vocabulary she needed to describe what she was in the process of doing. It helped her understand that fitting in is not the same as belonging, and that being yourself requires being brave enough to stand alone.

However, Ren had to learn how to stand alone because it was the complete opposite of what she had been doing her entire life. Growing up, she fought tooth and nail to fit in, be liked, and make everyone else happy so she didn't have to experience the pain of being alone, put down, or excluded ever again. But it turns out, this path was making her incredibly unhappy. To live the life of her dreams instead of the life expected of her, she had to have the courage to stand alone.

On her journey to reclaim her life, she had no idea what she was doing, and there was no guidebook. The journey was dark and murky, lonely and uncomfortable. She constantly questioned why she was doing it and whether the discomfort was worth it, but eventually, she could confidently stand alone. She started unapologetically doing what she wanted because it was right for her, even if it meant making others unhappy. The happiness she felt once she rebuilt her life in this way was beyond what she could have ever imagined for herself.

To stand alone, she learned you have to have the guts to go against the norm when everything screams to follow the crowd. It requires you to look fear in the eye and push forward anyway. You have to come to terms with disappointing others and understand that sometimes it's okay to be disliked or not fit in. You have to purposely bring temporary friction into your life when all you want is peace. And you have to walk into the unknown and hold *your breath to see if you'll come out better for it on the other side. Through this process, she learned that you do eventually come out on the other side to a life filled with genuine happiness.*

In the chapters that follow, you'll walk alongside Ren as she learns how to stand alone in a world of powerful and invisible social influence. You'll witness her moments of pain, fear, doubt, and courage, and watch her transform before your very eyes. You'll meet the friends Ren confided in and hear their stories, too, which inspired her along the way. Throughout, you'll also get a peek behind the curtain at the academic research that helped her make sense of her experiences and, ultimately, get her life back on track.

By the end, the hope is that your eyes will be opened, your mind will be challenged, your heart will be lifted, and you'll feel ready to embark on your own journey toward a life beyond what you ever imagined for yourself.

But first, we need to go back to when everything started to veer off track—Ren's childhood.

PART I
INWARD

CHAPTER ONE

POWERFUL AND INVISIBLE INFLUENCES

"Never mistake the power of influence."
-Jim Rohn

If you had asked Ren growing up whether she was easily influenced, she would have confidently said no. She thought of herself as independent—someone who made decisions based on her own wants and needs. However, she eventually discovered that this wasn't entirely true.

It turns out that it's easy to get swept up in living the life that's expected of us. There are thousands of powerful influences that impact the direction of our lives every single day. We are constantly being influenced, and it affects how we think, feel, and behave. Often, the pressure around us is so subtle and invisible that we don't even realize we're being nudged in a certain direction.

One of the biggest reasons we struggle to create the life of our dreams is because of the overwhelming and natural desire to belong. Deep down, we all just want to be loved and accepted, and we inherited this biological yearning from our ancestors 40,000 years ago. Back then, individuals belonged to small, intimate groups that provided for and kept each other safe. Our survival depended on being accepted within the group; going it alone was too risky, so we did whatever it took to belong.

As a result, our brains became naturally hardwired to try to fit in. We're programmed to follow the crowd and take the path of least resistance so we aren't rejected or excluded. Being excluded today isn't a matter of life or death like it was, but it can still be deeply painful. Our innate desire to fit in is still embedded in our DNA, consistently guiding our behavior and impacting every decision we encounter.

While it's naturally ingrained in us to try to fit in, our parents further emphasize this importance. As babies, we are our most authentic selves because societal norms and expectations have yet to influence us. As we age and develop, our parents begin to impose rules, values, beliefs, traditions, and expectations onto us long before we are even aware of it. Much of our life is decided for us, and we're expected to think, feel, and act in ways that align with our parents' expectations. We quickly learn to conform to these expectations to avoid letting our parents down or losing their admiration.

Then, we venture out into the world and attempt to live up to the expectations society has for us. When we're unsure how to act in a social situation, we use a mental shortcut called *social proof*. This means that we evaluate social norms by observing what everyone else is doing, and act accordingly by imitating the people around us. Imitating others causes many of us to become social chameleons, shapeshifting into personas different from who we truly are, often without even realizing it. We figure out what's popular or determine the "right" way to act and fall in line because it increases our chances of fitting in.

Social proof is wildly powerful and influential on our behaviors, decisions, and beliefs. Famous studies have shown that if everyone else is facing backward in an elevator, most people will eventually follow suit, even though they know it's not typical behavior. And if people give the wrong answer to a vision test with an obvious right answer, others will follow, giving the wrong answer too. People can recognize that certain behavior is not typical in a situation, but they'll still follow the crowd because they would rather be wrong and fit in than be right and stand out. If people can be swayed to follow the crowd when they know the behavior is blatantly incorrect, imagine the impact of less obvious influences on our day-to-day decisions and behavior without us realizing it.

Ren learned early in life what it felt like to not fit in, which only fueled her desire to belong even more. In first grade, she approached a group of kids playing soccer at recess, hoping to join in on the fun. The leader of the group—a girl named Mallory— stepped forward with her arms crossed and chin held high. "You can't play with us," Mallory said sharply, loud enough for everyone to hear. The other kids giggled nervously, clearly unwilling to challenge Mallory's authority. Ren quickly walked away to the other side of the schoolyard, where she sat alone and cried.

Being publicly rejected left a deep wound on her young heart. That day, she made an unspoken promise to herself: I'll never feel this way again. Instead of steering clear of Mallory, Ren worked tirelessly to gain her approval. Eventually, it worked—Mallory let her into the group. While the sting of exclusion faded, a new kind of discomfort took hold: the constant effort to appease Mallory—a textbook bully—so she wouldn't be cast aside again.

Over the years, the situation only worsened. Mallory would act like Ren's best friend one day, showering her with affection, only to cast her aside the next. She would invite the entire friend group out to dinner, deliberately leaving Ren at home in tears. Every other week, she'd post cryptic, passive-aggressive statuses about Ren or someone else in the group on social media. On one occasion, Mallory and a boy from school even stole Ren's boots and tossed them over a tall fence, forcing her to walk home in the dead of winter wearing only her socks while they snickered behind her. Each time Mallory tore her down, Ren desperately tried to claw her way back into being accepted.

Ren began developing social anxiety to the point it was making her physically ill. She confided in her mom but begged her not to intervene. "Mom, please don't! That's so embarrassing," she pleaded. Her mom agreed to find another way to help alleviate the stress. She bought Ren natural remedies to try to reduce her anxiety, and together they decided the best approach was to stay in Mallory's good graces, hoping she would eventually treat Ren kindly on a consistent basis.

Ren would take Mallory to sporting events, concerts, and even family vacations, trying to build a more genuine bond. It worked to a certain extent, but there were still cyclical highs and lows. While the highs were some of the greatest moments of Ren's life, and she deeply valued Mallory's friendship during those times, the lows were devastatingly soul-crushing.

As a result, Ren was constantly on edge. She became skilled at assessing everyone around her, evaluating what was socially acceptable, and adjusting her behavior accordingly. She grew attuned to people's unspoken expectations and even the subtlest shifts in their moods, allowing her to course-correct as needed. At school, she was a social chameleon, mirroring others and agreeing without hesitation to blend in seamlessly. She joined clubs and teams her friends preferred, even if they didn't interest her. She *followed trends she didn't care about and fawned over people who treated her poorly—all in a desperate pursuit of belonging.*

When Ren got to grad school, she finally started trying to make sense of her life by reading extensively. She came across research by Dr. Cristina Bicchieri, a philosopher and professor at the University of Pennsylvania, which helped her understand why people follow social norms. Ren read Dr. Bicchieri's book from start to finish, sometimes spending hours studying a single page. It was extremely technical and academic—definitely not meant to be a self-help book—but it helped Ren deeply understand her past and forge her future.

Dr. Bicchieri explains that we sometimes prefer to conform to social norms due to the following expectations: 1) most people close to us conform to the norm, and 2) most people close to us think we ought to conform to the norm as well.

A social norm

↳ is a rule of behavior

↳ that individuals prefer to conform to on the condition that they believe...

most people in their network conform to the social norm

most people in their network think they ought to conform to the social norm too

(Bicchieri, 2006)

We are constantly assessing what the people close to us do in certain situations, and notice what they think *others* should do in those situations, too. We pay close attention to the actions of the people we love and reflect on what they've done in the past. It becomes evident what people support or don't support, and we usually can't help but adjust accordingly. Knowing that everyone close to us does something and that they expect us to do it too provides an added layer of pressure when making decisions.

Depending on the choices we make, the people we love could either respond positively or negatively. When we follow a social norm, we are often greeted with positive reactions and approval. We are praised, celebrated, and well-liked when we do what is expected, resulting in positive relationships and feelings of warm acceptance. These positive interactions release dopamine, which our brains crave, making us want to replicate that feeling over and over again.

Our brains love predictability and knowing exactly what to do next, which is why we gravitate towards adopting social norms every chance we get. From a decision-making standpoint, following the crowd can actually be quite beneficial. We make approximately 35,000 decisions every single day, and falling back on norms gives us clear rules to follow. Doing so frees up brainpower to concentrate on more important decisions.

Just as we love following social norms, we equally loathe going against them. We worry that other people will react negatively to us if we go against the grain, and these worries can be real or perceived. Many times, even just the possibility of receiving negative reactions from people we care about is enough pressure to compel us to conform. When we go against a social norm, our brains emit a neurological error signal telling us that something is wrong which can stop us altogether.

If you thought our natural instinct to follow social norms wasn't strong enough already, being a people pleaser adds even more pressure to follow them. People pleasers tend to have painful childhood experiences of rejection, exclusion, or deprivation of love, resulting in a deep fear of abandonment. To counteract this fear, they try to gain love and affection by prioritizing other people's wants and needs above their own. Winning people's love and being liked causes a surge in dopamine, which trains our brains to continue doing what it takes to fit in and be liked. *This is exactly what happened to Ren with Mallory.*

All of these influences to follow the norm are incredibly powerful but can also be invisible if you aren't paying close attention, especially if you've never been taught to notice them. When we make decisions and evaluate which paths to take, it's easy to convince ourselves that we've been thoughtful and deliberate. However, the reality is that we are on autopilot most of the time, so we rarely realize there's a decision to make and end up unconsciously following societal norms without much deliberate thought.

We are instinctually being pulled toward the norm, which makes it feel like the natural and easy choice. The promised outcome of doing so is acceptance, being liked, and having what seems like positive relationships. Who doesn't want that? But we don't realize that following the norm when it doesn't align with our values can lead to an incredibly unhappy life. Continually making decisions based on the norm and what everyone else is doing—instead of what you truly want to do in life—can lead to an inauthentic, unfulfilling, and hollow existence with a silent veil of sadness. These feelings can be hard to detect due to the release of dopamine that you're getting from superficially fitting in.

When we follow norms that don't align with how we authentically want to live our lives, we end up following arbitrary norms that we don't believe in–simply because everyone else does or because it's expected of us. We start to limit ourselves by sacrificing our unique dreams just to stay on the path. We mold ourselves into someone we're not to fit into spaces we don't enjoy and do things we aren't interested in just to belong. Meanwhile, the people we meet along the way like us because of the false persona we've created, not because of the person we are within.

People's love for us is often conditional. They freely give us their love when we fulfill their expectations, add value to their lives, or minimize friction by sticking to the script like everyone else. We instinctively follow the crowd, unconsciously searching for the most coveted prize of all: genuine connection and belonging in this world. Unfortunately, this path often doesn't lead to those promised outcomes. People follow the norm, and once time has sufficiently passed them by, true belonging and happiness are often nowhere to be found.

By the time Ren was a sophomore in high school, she "fit in" by all accounts, but her social anxiety had become unbearable, overshadowing everything else. She often told her mom she wished she could move away and start over. One evening, her mom replied, "Well, my old boss has been after me to take a job up north, but I've never considered it because you'd have to switch schools." Ren's eyes lit up, and she agreed without hesitation. It was clear she had been deeply hurting for a long time and was desperate for a way out, which is why she was willing to make such a life-altering decision so quickly.

As soon as the school year ended, they packed up their family home and made the move. In her new surroundings, Ren began to thrive more than ever before. The difficult choice to uproot her life at the tender age of sixteen taught her an invaluable lesson: making hard decisions based on your true wants and needs can set you on a better path. However, old habits die hard. The behaviors she had adopted to appease those around her lingered, sabotaging her progress for years—until a fateful day in grad school, when she finally decided that enough was enough.

What most of us were never taught growing up is that it's actually the hard choice to go against the norm that leads to a truly happy life. It's the hard choice to stand alone when all you want to do is belong. It's the hard choice to face fear head-on instead of flinching and backing down. It's the hard choice to bring friction into your life when all you want is peace. It's the hard choice to jump into the unknown when all you want is certainty. It's making these hard choices consistently and over time that leads us to an authentic life filled with true belonging and genuine happiness.

Therefore, we need to ask ourselves as soon as possible in this life: Do you want easy choices now that lead to an unhappy life later? Or are you ready to make difficult choices now that lead to a happier life later on? When posed with these two options, which one would you choose?

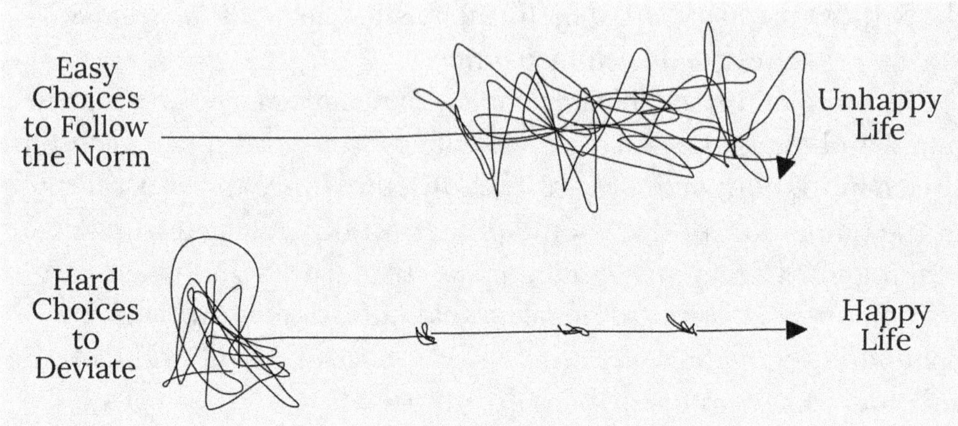

If you'd prefer–or are willing–to challenge yourself and make difficult choices now that lead to a happier life later, then you're in the right place. *Ren walked both of these paths, and is adamant that the easy choices to follow the crowd led her to deep unhappiness. It was the hard choices to go against the grain that brought her the genuine joy she feels today.*

Yes, the hard choices can be really, really challenging to make, which is why we often avoid them altogether. We waver on difficult decisions and talk ourselves out of them because it can feel scary. Our brains are actively trying to stop us from taking risks. So, how do we make the difficult choice of standing alone when everyone wants us to follow the crowd? To find out, we need to go back to when Ren was in grad school—a pivotal moment when everything started to change.

In summary...

• **Subtle influences shape our choices:** We may think we make independent decisions, but powerful social pressures often guide our thoughts and behaviors without us realizing it.

• **To belong, we often conform:** Humans have a deeply ingrained desire to belong, a trait inherited from our ancestors, which pushes us to conform to social norms, sometimes at the expense of authenticity.

• **Conformity can lead to a hollow existence:** Adapting to norms for social acceptance can lead to unhappiness if the decisions being made conflict with personal values, resulting in a life that may feel unfulfilling over time.

• **True happiness requires making the difficult choice to stand alone:** Genuine happiness comes from making choices that align with how you want to live—even if it means disappointing others.

Thought Starters

1. How do you feel about who you've become, how you spend your time, the people you surround yourself with, or the path you've taken in life?

2. How has your life path been positively and negatively influenced? Who influenced you along the way? Which influences have helped you in life, and which could you have gone without?

3. How have you challenged social norms in the past? When it comes to standing alone, what do you hope to learn and improve upon?

CHAPTER TWO

STAND ALONE

"It takes nothing to join the crowd.
It takes everything to stand alone."
-Hans F. Hansen

One evening, Ren sat cross-legged on her bed with a journal in hand, ready to reflect on her life. She was taking a much-needed night off from studying for exams and writing papers for grad school. She began with what seemed like a simple question: Who am I? As she stared at the blank page, her pen hovering above the paper, she froze and had no idea where to start.

She tapped her pen against the journal's edge, trying to think, but every answer that came to mind felt hollow. She thought about how she spent her time doing things she didn't enjoy, surrounded by people who didn't treat her well or friends with whom she had little in common. Although she didn't have a clear picture of who she was, she knew enough to realize she had been doing what was expected of her instead of what she truly wanted.

Ren came to the sobering realization that she had been going through the motions. Most decisions—big or small—had been based on what others thought or wanted, instead of what she truly felt. It was as though she had been sleepwalking through life, and now, she was fully awake. While shaken by her revelations, her next steps were clear: she needed to do what she wanted in life, just as her mom had told her during their final moments together. But *first, she needed to answer that simple question of who she was if she was ever going to start living for herself.*

To stand alone, we first need to take ourselves off autopilot and turn inward to better understand who we are at our core. Journaling—like Ren did—is a powerful way to become more mindful. We have to untangle who we want to be from the person we've been shaped into. What were you like when you were young, before all the influences in your life steered you this way and that? Who are you today, and who do you ultimately want to become? Once we know who we were, who we've been influenced into being, and who we want to become, we can get closer to becoming our true and ideal selves.

Not only do we need to understand who we are, but we also need to develop a deep understanding of our beliefs. Many times, our beliefs aren't clear or accessible to us on the surface because we're on autopilot or too focused on what's going on around us. Our unconscious beliefs have a profound impact on our behavior. Therefore, we have to become more aware by consciously evaluating our beliefs about how the world should be. Sometimes, when we examine these beliefs, we realize that our ideals are rooted in external influences more than we had previously thought.

For example, let's examine your beliefs about marriage. Perhaps you think you believe in the concept of marriage, or that you'd like to get married someday, but when you analyze that belief, you realize it stems from your childhood. If, when growing up, the only couples you interacted with were married, or your parents said things like, "One day when you get married..." you may have developed the belief that marriage is inevitable or necessary, instead of merely an option. Perhaps this idea was reinforced later in life because most of your friends got married too. Challenging our beliefs helps us understand more deeply what our actual preferences are, and you might find that you're perfectly content with not getting married, despite being conditioned to believe marriage is a given.

Once we know who we are and what our beliefs are, we can evaluate our lives through a new lens to make decisions that align with our actual desires and goals. To do so, it can be helpful to imagine we're sitting on a balcony observing ourselves. Look closely at the parts of your life that feel well-aligned with who you want to be, and recognize the parts that don't feel quite right. Assess if your current life is going to allow you to reach your ultimate hopes and dreams, and recognize areas of misalignment as opportunities for necessary change.

The good news is that we have the opportunity to alter the trajectory of our lives with every choice we make. When we're on autopilot, decisions pass us by without notice, and we end up making mindless turns that can take our lives off track. Being mindful helps us notice when opportunities for change and growth present themselves, allowing us to make intentional decisions about whether we want to follow or deviate from the norm.

People who deviate from the norm are willing to stand alone. Dr. Bicchieri refers to these individuals as "first movers"—those who make choices that differ from those around them. While they may not be the first to challenge a particular social norm, they are often among the first few in their social circle to do so.

When a norm doesn't align with their values, a first mover questions existing social norms, challenges the status quo, and discards arbitrary norms in favor of new ideas that better align with who they are and how they want to live.

Since choosing an alternate path is no easy feat, first movers tend to have important reasons for doing so. The most common reason is that a norm doesn't align with their personal values and beliefs. Following a norm they don't agree with would directly conflict with these beliefs, which is a non-negotiable and an important reason for going against a norm.

But just because a first mover deviates in one instance doesn't mean they will always do so. First movers can defy convention and adopt new behaviors when it comes to one social norm, but they might also sometimes conform to standards that align with their beliefs. The key is that they are willing to stand alone and choose a different path when a norm *doesn't* align with who they are and what they believe.

Several conditions must be met for a first mover to feel comfortable going against a social norm. *To help remember each condition outlined by Dr. Bicchieri, Ren created the acronym ALONE. While people aren't meant to be alone in theory, what Ren needed to learn most was how to stand alone in the face of social pressure, making the acronym especially fitting.*

Alter your path: Become less sensitive to what a norm represents and choose a different direction.

Lower the risk: Reduce and tolerate the risk.

Own your independence: Make decisions freely and independently, without external influence.

Nurture self-belief: Cultivate a deep belief in your ability to deviate.

Embrace the journey: Persevere and commit over time.

Alter Your Path

When first movers choose an alternate path, it's because they're less sensitive to what the norm stands for. Instead of blindly following the social norms they come into contact with and taking them for what they are, they question them. They assess what the norm is, where it originated from, what the norm represents, and so on. Someone sensitive to a norm can easily justify following it, while someone less sensitive sees no reason to follow a norm they don't believe in. While new information could shift first movers' opinions, how sensitive they are to a norm ultimately depends on their beliefs.

Lower the Risk

While low sensitivity to a norm is necessary for someone to go against it, first movers also have low perceived risk. Since norms are collectively approved by other people, deviating opens them up to negative reactions from others. First movers may face judgment, resistance, criticism, or even exclusion from those who want and expect them to follow the norm. These real and perceived risks strongly influence decisions about whether to go against a norm. So while someone might have less sensitivity to the norm, if the risk seems too high, it may cause them to conform. Alternatively, someone with low perceived risk has evaluated the potential consequences and is willing to take the risk.

Own Your Independence

Another essential condition for first movers to go against a norm is independence. First movers make decisions independently without being controlled or influenced by anyone else. They are able to withstand the pressures from loved ones and society to conform. Even when facing pressure, they will hold strong and continue on with their decisions.

Nurture Self-Belief

Lastly, first movers believe in themselves and their ability to deviate from a norm. Making the difficult decision to stand alone can result in a lot of discomfort, but first movers don't let that stop them. Instead, they face negative reactions from those they care about head on. First movers have to believe that they can handle whatever comes their way and that their decisions will lead to a beneficial outcome while they actively deviate from a norm.

Embrace the Journey

When all of these conditions are met, first movers gain the confidence to go against the grain. Truly embracing the journey means committing to the process over time. One small act of deviance can build the confidence to do it again. The more you challenge the norm when it feels right, the easier the journey becomes—though it will never be entirely free of discomfort. Ultimately, you become more comfortable with being uncomfortable, more mindful than not, and you begin to consistently make decisions rooted in your beliefs, wants, and needs, which start to feel like second nature.

However, when one of these key ingredients is missing, it can make the difference between someone deviating from the norm or following it. It's possible that someone may be sensitive to a certain norm and convince themselves to follow it. Maybe the real or perceived risk is too great to bear. Perhaps they succumb to peer pressure or don't believe in their ability to go against the norm. Strengthening your abilities in each of these areas is key to becoming a first mover with the courage to stand alone.

After a lot of reflection, Ren developed a deeper understanding of who she wanted to become and the life she wanted to create. Her aspirations were different from her friends' or family's, so she knew in order to achieve her dreams, she'd have to make quite a few decisions that were counter to what her loved ones expected. This intimidated her, and it took her a while before she was able to stand alone like first movers do.

Once she had a clear vision on who she wanted to become, what her beliefs were, and how she wanted to live, she grew less sensitive to the norms around her, but still never deviated from those norms because she was constantly appeasing people, falling to peer pressure, and too worried about what others might think. Decades of going along with what everyone else wanted don't just disappear overnight. Often, the potential consequences of deviating from the norm felt too risky, and she doubted whether she had the courage or strength to follow through.

However, she recognized that she wanted to break away from the norm, so she set out to go against the grain and work towards autonomy every day. Moving farther away from home for grad school was her first big step towards independence. It gave her the freedom to make decisions for herself, and she found it easier to go against the grain, say no, and set boundaries when surrounded by people she barely knew.

Over time, she began to believe in her ability to deviate and stopped giving in to peer pressure as much. She repeated this process until it became more natural to confidently stand behind her decisions. Eventually, she started applying what she had practiced to her relationships and experiences back home. She made choices that were right for her and, little by little, she began to reclaim her life and feel happier.

In summary...

• **Mindfulness allows us to make more intentional life choices:** By being present and taking ourselves off autopilot, we can evaluate our current experiences and make more deliberate decisions.

• **Understanding yourself opens up room for authenticity:** To live authentically, it's crucial to reflect deeply on your true self, stepping into who you want to be instead of the person society has conditioned you to be.

• **Challenging our core beliefs helps clarify personal desires:** Examining beliefs, especially those formed from external influences, helps reveal whether they align with personal values or not.

• **"First movers" stand alone:** They choose an **A**lternate path, **L**ower the risk, **O**wn their independence, **N**urture self-belief, and **E**mbrace the journey.

Thought Starters

1. What were you like when you were young, before influences impacted your life? Who have you been influenced into being today and who do you want to ultimately become?

2. Which parts of your life are aligned with who you'd ideally like to be and which parts don't feel quite right?

3. What's one decision you could make today to get your life more aligned with who you hope to be?

CHAPTER THREE

CONVEY, SWAY, AND STAY

*"If you would persuade, you must appeal
to interest rather than intellect."*
–Benjamin Franklin

Deciding to stand alone and go against the grain is a feat in itself, but what Ren struggled with the most was communicating these plans to her loved ones. She had always made decisions that pleased those around her, so making choices that differed from what others expected–and that risked upsetting or disappointing people–was excruciatingly hard for her. It was uncharted territory she had never navigated before, but she knew she needed to learn how to do it as best she could.

Ren's journey began with small, quiet acts of rebellion. She started by turning down invitations from her new friends in grad school when she didn't feel like going out. "Thanks for the invite, but I'm going to stay in and study tonight," she'd text. Ren worried about declining, remembering her mom's warnings from childhood that saying no could cause people to stop inviting her. But her friends' responses were encouraging: "No worries! There's always next weekend," they'd reply. Each time she made a decision based on her own needs—and the world didn't fall apart—she felt a small sense of relief, and her confidence began to grow.

She took a bigger step by breaking from holiday traditions, especially those involving her father, with whom she had a strained relationship. Since her mother's passing, there was no longer a reason to go home for the holidays. Ren told her dad she was too busy with work to visit, but the truth was she wanted to celebrate on her own. Unable to share her true reasons, she told a small lie—that she would make it next year—to soften the blow. Deep down, however, she knew she had no intention of spending the holidays with him again.

At first, Ren's approach to setting boundaries wasn't ideal. She avoided hard conversations, choosing the quiet path of no explanations and no confrontation. She would write people off without telling them why, cancel plans last minute with flimsy excuses, and drift away from relationships that no longer served her without closure. She knew this wasn't fair to the people on the other end, but it was her training ground—a place to learn how to disappoint others without letting their feelings dictate her actions.

And it worked. Each silent decision and boundary she enforced without an explanation strengthened her. Slowly, she realized that the weight of someone's disappointment wasn't as heavy as she'd imagined. With every choice she made for herself, she grew sturdier and less shaken by others' opinions.

When Ren finally had a solid foundation beneath her, she began to approach her communication differently and in a more productive way. From that point on, Ren found herself having more candid conversations. When her family asked if she was coming home for the holidays, she explained her plans clearly. When friends pushed her to hang out when she didn't want to, she thanked them genuinely and declined without hesitation.

Each conversation reaffirmed what she had learned in those early, silent rebellions: the world didn't crumble when she made decisions based on what she wanted—even if they were counter to what others expected. And now, with her newfound strength, she *no longer needed to hide her choices in the shadows. She could stand firm in her decisions, face the discomfort head-on, negotiate for what she needed, and make compromises when it felt right— one choice, one boundary, one candid conversation at a time.*

The moment you share your intentions to go against the grain, you bring these decisions to life, opening yourself up to varied opinions, judgments, or criticisms. This is a pivotal moment where you can face fear head-on, lean into the discomfort, communicate your plans, navigate conflict that arises, and withstand peer pressure, all while trying to keep your relationships intact.

It's a difficult part of the process, but since our decisions often impact others, it's essential to communicate our intention to deviate from the norm. Our lives are an elaborate, interconnected network of parents, siblings, extended relatives, and friends we might want to consider, and our decisions affect their lives in big and small ways. Instead of making choices in a vacuum, it's crucial to communicate our plans effectively so we can help soften our loved ones' reactions, garner their much-needed support, and keep our bonds with them strong.

In an ideal world, we'd communicate our plans to go against the grain, and our loved ones would be quick to offer unconditional love and support. Realistically, however, going against the norm can cause negative reactions ranging from judgment, criticism, gossip, and scolding to withholding love. People struggle with our decisions to deviate from the norm because doing so challenges their beliefs and expectations. Additionally, our unconventional decisions might inconvenience, stress, or detract from the enjoyment of their lives, which can be upsetting, regardless of how much they love us.

Since we cannot escape the intertwined nature of our social networks, we need to find ways to balance living how we want while maintaining relationships with those close to us. We can't deviate from social norms with zero consideration for other people's feelings and expect everyone to understand or support our decisions. Alternatively, we can't prioritize what others want over our needs. A happy medium exists, allowing us to pursue our desires while being considerate of our loved ones and upholding our relationships.

When we share our plans to deviate from the norm with those close to us, three grounding principles can help ensure a positive outcome: convey, sway, and stay. We must convey essential information about our plans to friends and family. When communicating these details, we need to persuade them and sway our loved ones to see our point of view so they'll be more apt to support our decisions. And lastly, regardless of their reactions, we must stay firm in our decision to make choices that serve us best.

When we convey a decision we've made to the people close to us, direct and honest communication is key. We might be tempted to water down our explanation of a decision to make other people feel more comfortable. Avoid beating around the bush or sugarcoating your intentions, since this could detract from your overall message. Skipping information, withholding details, or convoluting the message could make them feel blindsided later on if they feel like they didn't have the full picture. Make sure the people close to you have a complete understanding of what you plan to do so they can manage their own expectations.

To get friends and loved ones to support us in our decisions to go against the norm, we need to sway them to see our point of view. Just because you are close with someone doesn't mean they hold the same beliefs and outlook on life, which is why we need to help these people understand our perspective before we stand alone. Communicating the rationale behind our decision to go against the norm is essential, and can help persuade friends and family to support our decisions, making these choices much more joyful.

Persuading people that a decision is right for you begins with trust, which gets built long before you even have to communicate about your decision to go against a norm. People who trust you are more willing to listen to you and perceive your words and actions as credible. Building trust and credibility with the people close to you increases the likelihood that they'll be willing to listen and hear you out.

Once we've built trust, it can be helpful to first share our plans to go against the norm with the people we trust the most. Doing so creates a safe space to communicate our plans–and the rationale behind them–for the first time. We can talk candidly about our goals, get feedback, and become more comfortable telling people about what we want to do. Additionally, once our most trusted confidantes are on board, they can help champion our plan to go against the norm and garner other people's support. Then, we can go on to tell the more sensitive individuals in our lives who might have more adverse reactions.

Knowing what those close to us value most can help us communicate our plan to go against the norm in a way that resonates. This way, we can emphasize the benefits of our decision, draw similarities between what we want to do and what they've done in the past, or explain our plan based on widely accepted values or the personal values of whoever we're talking to. It's much easier to convince people to accept and support us if we can point out how our decisions are consistent with what they're already doing or how they think and feel.

Since we're reframing our "rebellion" to make it more palatable, we need to stay rooted in our values and beliefs to avoid losing the integrity of any plans. Once someone starts to get on board with your decision, you can boost their confidence in you by letting them know of other people's support. People like knowing they feel similarly and are on the same page as others. Being aligned with the majority gives many people social validation and makes them feel much more confident in an idea, too.

If we suspect that someone might be particularly resistant to our decision to swim upstream, we can make the conversation less tense by reminding them that we're on the same team. Instead of framing the decision around yourself, you can use more cooperative language focused on "we" and "us" to help them see your point of view and increase their interest in wanting to work towards a positive solution together.

Upon informing the people closest to you about your plans to deviate from the norm, you may face counter arguments and negative reactions—some may even try to talk you out of your decisions. Hear them out and try to understand where they are coming from, but be prepared to confidently counter their objections and continue to build the case for why the decision is right for you. In some cases, you may even want to prepare for the relationship to rupture or face strain. You can do your part to make repairs, but it's always possible that your decisions to do things differently is more than a loved one is willing to handle. Stay strong and try not to cave when things get tense.

It's inevitable that when we listen to our loved ones, they might surprise us with counter arguments that make us reconsider. Whether they present new information or cause you to shift your perspective a bit, you may find room for a compromise. Finding a "happy medium" or middle ground can be an amazing option, especially when you can do so in a way that feels comfortable and aligned with your overall vision and goals.

While we need to be mindful of how our decisions impact those around us, some people are stuck in their ways and will never see your point of view. Even if you communicate your plans to deviate from the norm in a mature, empathetic, and thoughtful way, these people might still respond by acting out, guilting you, or making you feel bad about your decision. Suppose they strongly oppose your decision while being unwilling to work toward repairing the relationship. In that case, we must hold firm in our decision regardless of their feelings. We can't appease people who are difficult or unwilling to consider our point of view.

Once you've come to a final decision that aligns with how you want to live your life and you've communicated your plans to your friends and family, you can step into that decision with confidence. Decisions that align with our values, beliefs, and goals feel better than those that don't, and we're less likely to regret and revert those choices. Let the dust settle, and be proud that you made the difficult decision to stand alone.

In summary...

• **We must balance authenticity with maintaining relationships:** Sharing your decision to go against social norms with loved ones can be challenging but is essential. It helps manage their reactions and fosters their support.

• **Effective communication and persuasion is essential:** To encourage understanding and support, be direct and honest, build trust, and use empathetic language. Relating your decision to shared values or others' past experiences can make it more relatable.

• **Standing firm in our decisions amid resistance:** Be prepared for counterarguments and potential strain on relationships. Stay true to your decision, even if some loved ones find it difficult to accept or support you.

Thought Starters

1. How do you feel about how your friends and family communicate with each other? What do you like and what could be improved?

2. Who do you feel most comfortable sharing personal stories and updates with? Who do you struggle to open up with and why?

3. What's one action you can take today to improve communication with your friends and family?

CHAPTER FOUR

HEART OF THE MATTER

> "Sometimes we create our own
> heartbreak with expectations."
> -Unknown

Ren had spent much of her life feeling weighed down by others' expectations. People assumed she would seamlessly fit into their plans and eagerly join their activities. While she had started declining invitations that didn't align with how she wanted to spend her time, she realized this approach wasn't sustainable. Her mother had been right: if you decline enough invitations, people will eventually stop extending them, so Ren knew she needed a better solution.

She realized the problem stemmed from a lack of clarity—everyone still saw the old Ren, who had always mirrored the interests of those around her. People were used to her fulfilling their expectations because that was what she had always done. If she wanted to reclaim her life, she needed to show them who she truly was. This meant openly sharing about herself so they could better understand what they could realistically expect from her.

Instead of letting life passively unfold, Ren decided to take control by helping shape her loved ones' expectations. She began weaving her preferences and values into conversations with friends and family over time. Gradually, her openness began to transform her relationships. Her friends started tailoring their *invitations to match her interests. Instead of suggesting loud concerts or crowded bar crawls, they invited her to morning hikes or quiet dinners. And when they extended an invitation that didn't quite match her style, they completely understood if she politely declined.*

Ren started to feel a deep sense of peace in her relationships. By being honest about who she was and what she needed, she had cultivated connections where she could truly be herself. Her friends didn't just tolerate her boundaries; they respected and embraced them. Ren realized that by sharing more of herself, she made it easier for others to meet her where she was. She no longer carried the burden of trying to meet expectations she couldn't realistically fulfill. Instead, she co-created deep and honest connections with friends—one candid conversation at a time.

While effectively communicating our plans to deviate from the norm is essential, shaping our loved ones' expectations to be more realistic is key when standing alone. We all have expectations; it's a natural part of life. However, unrealistic expectations cause unnecessary conflict in our lives. We assume most people will think and behave similarly to us, leading to ill-conceived expectations based on those assumptions. Then, we mindlessly and silently place these expectations onto our partners, children, friends, family, and colleagues.

We build up expectations for the people around us because it helps us navigate the uncertainty of the future. However, people inevitably fall short or behave differently than we anticipate since many don't think, feel, or act exactly as we do. This is what happens when people go against social norms; going against the grain doesn't align with what others expect, causing friction in relationships. When our expectations don't materialize in real life and produce different or less favorable circumstances than we expected, we tend to have emotional reactions.

While it's okay to feel emotional in the face of unmet expectations, we need to learn how to effectively cope with negative feelings that arise. Several researchers propose three ways to cope with unfulfilled expectations: assimilation (taking steps to ensure one's expectations are met in the future), accommodation (adapting previous expectations to align with the actual outcome), or immunization (devaluing or reframing the meaning of the unfulfilled expectation). It is our responsibility to cope with negative emotions that come from unrealized expectations without putting guilt, blame, or shame on those who don't fulfill them.

When expectations don't pan out, we need to figure out when to adapt and when to hold firm. Figuring out why our expectations were left unfulfilled allows us to learn and adapt to be more realistic in the future. However, sometimes our expectations aren't met due to random factors outside of our control. Other times, we might have expectations about how other people should treat us (e.g., fairly and respectfully), and just because people don't meet them doesn't mean we should adjust our expectations or accept poor treatment. Constantly reflecting on why our hopes or desires didn't materialize can help us learn and understand when to adjust and when to hold strong.

One of the best ways to help the people in our lives develop more realistic expectations of us is by sharing more openly about our authentic selves. When those close to us understand our values, interests, and beliefs, they can better anticipate our behavior. While we can share who we are, we can't force people to listen or accept ideas outside their own realities. There's no guarantee they will adjust their expectations, but it usually doesn't hurt to try.

Vice versa, we can develop more realistic expectations for the people around us by simply getting to know them better, too. To do so, we need to connect with them directly, engage in conversation, and get to know their unique perspectives. What are their interests and preferences? How do they view the world? How do they like to spend their time? What's their personality like? How do they react when things don't go their way? Knowing more about a person and how they consistently think and feel helps us develop a clearer picture of what we can realistically expect from them.

However, getting to know someone on a deeper level isn't always possible, so we have to find other ways to reframe our expectations. Maybe the communication lines aren't open, or there isn't an opportunity to get to know someone better. In such cases, we should avoid making too many assumptions about who people are and what to expect from them, since guessing doesn't always pan out. Regardless of whether you know someone intimately or not, we can assume that people will try to make the best decisions they can for themselves. It might not be a decision we agree with or would make in the same situation, but we can appreciate that the decision is theirs to make, and trust they made the right choice for them.

One area of life where people need realistic expectations is how others spend their time. Time is our most valuable, finite resource, and people are always vying for it. We often ask those we care about for their time: "Hey, do you want to grab dinner sometime this week?" or "I was hoping to come into town this weekend, can I stay at your place?" When we bring a proposition to someone, we've put them in a position to say yes or no; and we're hoping they say yes, which adds social pressure. However, constantly saying yes can quickly cause our schedules to get overrun by what everyone else wants to do, leaving no time for ourselves.

Since we are not entitled to anyone's time, we have to be more thoughtful about making these requests, especially since saying no is difficult for many. Adding "no pressure" to the end of our propositions can help alleviate some stress by signaling that it's okay to say no and reassuring them we'll still love them, regardless of whether they meet our expectations. Just like we welcome other people telling us no, we must become more confident in saying no to propositions as well.

Furthermore, when we agree to spend time with others, we need to ensure upfront that our expectations align. Many of us maintain unspoken or ambiguous beliefs about what should happen in a given situation, leading to potential conflict when differing expectations collide. Two people could have the same itinerary but completely different goals of how to spend time. Depending on how things play out, someone's expectations might be fulfilled while the other person's are not. Establishing clarity upfront is critical; open and honest conversations help align expectations so everyone can spend the time together in a mutually fulfilling way.

When people maintain realistic expectations and give people grace when they fall short, it creates a safer space for everyone to step into who they want to become. In contrast, unrealistic expectations constrict and restrict people from living how they want. When we're more forgiving and place less pressure on loved ones to meet our expectations, we give them the space to live more authentically without the worry of letting us down

This approach helps us create a more peaceful existence and avoid getting worked up about how others choose to live.

In summary...

• **Manage expectations to reduce friction**: Recognize and adjust unrealistic expectations to avoid conflict, especially when others' actions differ from what we might assume.

• **Develop coping strategies for unmet expectations**: Use methods like trying to have your expectations met next time, adapting expectations, or reframing unmet expectations to handle disappointments constructively.

• **Communicate openly for realistic relationships**: Share your authentic self and actively learn about others to develop more accurate expectations, fostering stronger, more understanding connections.

• **Respect time and boundaries**: Be thoughtful with requests for time, clearly communicate intentions, and be open to both giving and receiving "no" as an answer to create balanced, respectful relationships.

Thought Starters

1. What are some current expectations your friends and family have of you? Do you feel these are realistic or not? How do these expectations make you feel?

2. What should friends and family realistically expect from you? How does this differ from or align with the expectations they place on you?

3. How can you help your loved ones develop more realistic expectations about who you are, the decisions you make, and how you spend your time?

PART II
OUTWARD

FIRST MOVERS

"[First movers] will never influence their peers if news of their deviance does not spread."
-Dr. Cristina Bicchieri

When Ren began to get her life back on track, she struggled to figure out her unique path—and how to walk it—because she had never done it before and didn't have many people to turn to for guidance. She didn't personally know anyone going against the norm or living the life she dreamed of. So, she started navigating the path on her own, which was an incredibly lonely journey.

While we often see people following societal norms and openly sharing their experiences, it's much harder to find examples of those who go against the grain. First movers—people who challenge norms and forge new paths—are more difficult to identify because their stories aren't told as often or as loudly. Even when first movers find the courage to defy norms, they sometimes keep their stories and experiences to themselves to avoid judgment.

Ren had to confront and challenge many social norms that didn't feel right for her. Along the way, she shared her life stories with the people she trusted most. To her surprise, the more Ren shared, the more others opened up about similar experiences. She realized there were plenty of first movers living alongside her—

they just didn't typically talk openly about their decisions to go against the grain until someone else breached the topic first.

These conversations were invaluable. Ren laughed and cried with people from all walks of life. They validated each other's feelings and walked away from those deep discussions feeling less alone. Some of these individuals were strangers she had just met; others were people she had known for years but had no idea about the life stories hidden beneath the surface. It wasn't that Ren couldn't be trusted—it was that these experiences had been kept locked away, rarely shared with anyone.

The next six chapters challenge some social norms prevalent in Western society today, inviting you to reevaluate—or reaffirm— deeply ingrained beliefs about home life, family, marriage, how we spend our time, what we prioritize, and more. It's worth noting that these social norms aren't inherently good or bad, right or wrong. Just because this book dissects and challenges them doesn't mean you need to go against them. There's a long list of norms that could have been addressed, but this book focuses on the ones Ren and her friends wrestled with.

Ultimately, the most important lesson woven throughout these pages is that the choice of how to live is always yours to make. Whether these stories resonate with you or not, the purpose of questioning these norms is to encourage you to think critically about the world around you and the expectations we often follow by default. By doing so, we can make more informed decisions about our own paths. These stories are shared with the hope of inspiring you to reflect on your choices and feel confident in standing alone as you pursue the path that suits you best.

CHAPTER FIVE

GOING THE DISTANCE

"Leave home with a big, bright dream.
Nurture it into a bigger, brighter reality."
-Unknown

Ren had always dreamed of going far away for college—somewhere completely new where she could reinvent herself. But when the acceptance letters started rolling in, the thought of leaving her mom behind felt overwhelming. Her mom had always been her rock, a source of comfort in a home often overshadowed by her father's brooding presence. The idea of being states away from her was too much to bear. So, Ren chose a school just three hours from her hometown—a manageable drive whenever she needed to see her mom.

At first, staying close felt like the right choice. Ren could visit her mom on weekends, going on long drives together where their heartfelt talks felt like therapy. But as time went on, Ren began to feel like she'd never truly left home. Expectations still loomed over her from old friends, relatives, and her father. The proximity made it too easy for people to pull her back into obligations she didn't want to fulfill—attending events she had no interest in and conforming to who she had always been in their eyes.

Ren realized that, although she was away at college, she wasn't really free. She yearned for something more—a chance to break *away from the confines of her familiar world and discover who she was on her own terms.*

After her mother passed away, Ren made the bold decision to move across the country for grad school—far enough away that she could no longer feel the gravitational pull of her hometown. For the first time in her life, Ren was untethered. In her new city, she didn't know anyone, and no one knew her. There were no expectations, no preconceived notions, no obligations. It was just her, alone with the freedom to figure out who she was.

At first, being far away from home was daunting. She cried herself to sleep most nights, overwhelmed by the discomfort and loneliness. Ren had to navigate a new city, build a life from scratch, and learn how to set boundaries with people she barely knew. But those experiences were life-changing, and over time, she learned how to live for herself rather than for others.

Over the years, Ren moved back and forth across the country several times, each move teaching her something new about herself. She discovered an appreciation for the desert, a love for hiking in the Pacific Northwest, a knack for writing in a small coastal town in California, and a passion for classical music in New York City. With every relocation, she felt like she was shedding layers of who she had been expected to be and stepping closer to the person she truly was.

Looking back, Ren didn't regret staying close to home for college; it had given her the comfort she needed at that point in her life and valuable time with her mother before she passed. But moving away had been a turning point. It allowed her to break free from external influences and chart her own path. She learned the value of setting boundaries, the joy of self-discovery, and the beauty of living life authentically.

As she worked to get her life back on track, she often reflected on a quote from Cornelia Parker: "You only get one life, so it seems to me you might as well do the things you want to do." From the moment she moved away, she began doing exactly what she wanted with her one life—just as her mom had encouraged her to do.

Deciding where to live is usually one of the more impactful decisions of your life. Each place has its distinct culture, traditions, dialect, values, people, and geographical landscape. These factors can influence how we experience the world, who we become, and how we spend our time. Where we live has a powerful impact on our overall health and happiness, so settling down or relocating is a decision that demands thoughtfulness and intentionality.

It's important to note that if you are in a position to contemplate where you want to live, and have the means to make the move a reality, you are coming from a place of privilege. Some people aren't able to choose where they live because uprooting and moving to a new place requires the flexibility or financial means to do so. Therefore, the sentiment of intentionally choosing where to live to maximize our health and happiness may not be possible for all, and this should be taken into consideration throughout the chapter.

Even if you are able to intentionally decide where to live, moving is often easier said than done due to the interconnected nature of life, family, work, and relationships. Throughout our childhood, where we live is influenced by our family—we live where our parents or caregivers have chosen to live. And it could be that our parents chose to live where their parents lived, too. But once we become an adult, we get to make decisions about where to put down roots. This decision often comes about when we're going to college, beginning our careers, or starting a family, and many end up deciding to stay put, maintaining close proximity to loved ones.

In America, about 6 in 10 young adults live within a 10-mile radius of their hometown, with 8 in 10 living within 100 miles of where they grew up. Even the opportunity to earn higher wages in cities located farther away isn't enough to alter these trends. The decision to live close to family is consistent with older Americans too; the typical American lives about 18 miles from their mom. Over the decades, Americans have stayed closer to "home" with most adults not venturing too far from where they grew up.

If you have healthy and stable relationships, there are benefits to living in close proximity to family and friends. You get to maintain closer connections with them than you would if you lived farther away. You get to see and experience their important milestones in life. You get to grow together throughout the years and enjoy quality time together. These positive social interactions and having a tight-knit community can be crucial for our well-being and longevity. And if your hometown aligns with the person you want to become and the life you want to live, then it's a win-win: you get to live authentically while spending time with the people you love as well.

Living close to home gives you access to a built-in community, which can be helpful from a financial perspective as well. Many young adults decide to live close to family because they can save money on rent, laundry, meals, and groceries. Older adults often move closer to home once they have kids to experience these financial benefits, since their parents are able to help with childcare and chores. Additionally, we're able to look after and care for our parents in the final stretch of their life instead of paying for caregiving services from afar. Being able to share and pool resources with our family can help alleviate financial stressors, and makes living close to "home" a huge benefit.

While there are many benefits to living close to family, depending on your situation, there might also be drawbacks. We tend to form connections and relationships with those who we are physically close to, which is called the proximity principle. We are born into our family and then live in close proximity to them because of that familial bond. Our entire social network then largely becomes predicated on proximity. However, sometimes those relationships can be unstable or unhealthy, which can lead to negative interpersonal connections. If the people that surround us aren't good influences or cause us stress, then it can greatly impact our mental health.

Staying in our hometown could potentially hold us back from accomplishing our dreams and reaching our full potential as well. When our hometown is the only way of life we know, our hopes and dreams start to revolve around what's possible within that context. We can climb the ladder or learn as much as possible, but we'll eventually hit a ceiling. What we don't see are the opportunities and possibilities that exist beyond the boundaries of our hometown. If we don't step outside of the confines of where we're from, we might not ever see what we're truly capable of.

Staying where we grew up can stifle our curiosity and limit exploration. When we live in the same place for extended periods of time, we fall into predictable routines—we take our usual route to work and go to the same grocery stores, restaurants, and local shops. Our ancestors used to search for answers by exploring unknown lands, but when we have the same routines in familiar places, our only outlet for exploration becomes searching for answers online. We rarely get to feed our curiosity in our day-to-day lives by exploring unfamiliar worlds, which can be unfulfilling for some and cause time to pass us by in the blink of an eye.

While there are pros and cons of living close to home, what might happen if we decided to live somewhere different or new? It can be hard to make that decision, especially if the people close to us have expectations about where we belong. If most people we know live close to family, and the people we care about think we ought to live close to family too, there's a chance that we choose to follow the norm instead of challenging the status quo.

While the expectations of other people can be influential in our decisions about where to live, emotional ties can keep us close to home as well. When we live somewhere for a significant amount of time, become well-established in our community, and create a solid social circle, we develop an emotional attachment to that place. Additionally, we tend to unconsciously give preference to people and places we're familiar with, so the emotional attachment and comfort we have with our hometown can influence us to stay close to home.

As a result of this emotional attachment, we can become skeptical of stepping outside of our comfort zone, which can hinder growth and development. Our hometown becomes favorable because it's familiar, safe, and secure. A predictable routine keeps us relatively even-keeled, minimizing anxiety and worry. However, this can cause us to burrow deeper into our comfort zone, even if it's not the best for us, and prevent us from pursuing other opportunities that will allow us to grow and transform.

The act of moving away can be hard, too. Uprooting your life and settling into an unfamiliar place is not an easy process. Relocations can be a very stressful life event—not only is it logistically challenging, but moving away also distances us from the people and places we love. Moving requires us to leave family, friends, and sometimes jobs behind. All of this can provoke negative emotions, such as anxiety, loneliness, sadness, hopelessness, and fear of a new beginning. Not wanting to experience these uncomfortable emotions or stresses can keep many from making a move, even if it would benefit them in the long run.

While moving can be hard, it can be good for us too. Venturing outside of our hometown broadens our horizon and opens our eyes to what's possible in this world. When we're exposed to new places and possibilities, our hopes and dreams start to evolve and expand beyond what we thought was possible for ourselves, allowing us to stretch and reach our full potential. We have to make new friends and build a new community for ourselves, which challenges us in new ways. It gets us outside of our predictable routines, gives us the excitement of exploring new and unknown places, and slows time down since we can't operate on autopilot.

Moving can give you a fresh start and allow you to become your true self. When we are no longer surrounded by people who have known us forever and are in a new environment, we can feel freer to change our habits and adapt who we are, giving us a chance to live more authentically.

There's a lot to consider when deciding where to live, but the journey should begin by assessing whether your current living situation aligns with your aspirations. It's important to reflect on your own life in order to decide where you're meant to be.

When Ren moved away for grad school, she didn't have many friends to confide in. Most of the people she knew had stayed close to home, leaving her with few who could truly empathize with the changes she was experiencing. However, at school, she was surrounded by others who had relocated—just like she had.

As Ren was settling into her apartment, her new roommate, Lucy, walked through the door. They chatted for a bit, exchanging stories about where they were from and what they were studying. Lucy mentioned that she had just driven eight hours from her hometown to get there and didn't know anyone in the area either. While they both felt uneasy about being so far from home for the first time, they felt comforted knowing they had each other.

After Lucy unpacked her belongings, reality set in—she was alone in an unfamiliar place. Her new journey began with tears, fear, and discomfort. All she could do was take it one step at a time, trying to build a temporary new life for herself. At first, she expected to be gone for just a year—long enough to earn her graduate degree before returning home as if nothing had changed. But as time passed, she realized she was likely never going back to stay.

She finished grad school the following year and moved again—this time even farther from home. The emotions she felt were similar to her last move: she was alone and sad all over again. But just like before, she began to build a new life, and the sadness eventually gave way to genuine happiness. That wouldn't be the last time she moved, either. Lucy uprooted her life and relocated three more times after that, with each move feeling a little less scary and a lot more rewarding.

The biggest thing Lucy noticed about moving away was the sense of freedom it brought. For the first time, she felt like she had a blank canvas in front of her, with creative direction entirely in her hands. She was free from obligations, expectations, and the influence of others. This gave her the opportunity to learn, grow, evolve, dream, and create the life she wanted. That freedom was truly liberating.

While the freedom was liberating, being away from her mom was heartbreaking. Lucy and her mom shared an incredibly special bond, and it hurt that they couldn't spend more time together. But being away, she had learned that she wasn't meant to stay in her hometown. She coped with the pain of being apart by visiting her mom as often as possible and sharing her beautiful new life with her.

Losing touch with people who had once been her best friends was another painful reality. Lucy did her best to stay connected, but some relationships naturally faded over time. It was difficult to return home and feel like she no longer belonged, or to accept that some friends had no intention of visiting or being part of her new life. However, these losses were gradually replaced with new, deeper connections—like her friendship with Ren—and, despite the distance, these relationships transcended time and space.

Living far from her hometown is bittersweet, but Lucy wouldn't trade the experience for anything. It allowed her to create a life beyond her wildest dreams, grow in ways she never thought possible, and cultivate the most fulfilling relationships of her life. While it's sad that some friendships didn't withstand the distance and that she doesn't see her mom as often as she'd like, her life is incredibly beautiful and filled with so much joy. Life is good—and it's all because she had the courage to move away.

After graduation, Ren and Lucy moved to different states to pursue their careers but kept in touch. Over the years, both relocated to various cities across the U.S. Though their surroundings constantly changed, their bond remained strong. During one of Ren's moves, she spent about a year in San Francisco, where she met Kat, who had recently relocated to the Bay Area from the Midwest. It was Kat's first time living farther away from home, where she had spent most of her life.

At first, Kat was reluctant to move and only considered it after her husband urged her to think about it seriously. He frequently traveled to the West Coast for work, which led him to suggest relocating to San Francisco. Her immediate reaction was, "Why would I do that? My family is nearby, my friends are here, my life is here." He pushed back, saying, "You know you don't have to live the same life your parents did, right?" Taken aback, she replied, "What do you mean?!" In her mind, that was the only option.

Growing up in the Midwest, she was taught to stay close to home and follow a certain path: attend college, find a partner, get a job, buy a house, and start a family. And the sooner these milestones were achieved, the better. Her parents were high school sweethearts who had built a wonderful life for themselves by following these unspoken rules passed down by society and their own parents. Kat was excited to emulate their choices, believing it was the key to a happy life.

After graduating from college, Kat moved to Chicago with her boyfriend, who would later become her husband. Her new home was still relatively close to her family, and she remained committed to following a more traditional path. She landed her dream job at Wrigley and fully expected to spend the rest of her career there. She and her boyfriend married young and began diligently saving for their future home. She could envision their next steps: settling into their first house together and having multiple children by the time they were 30.

But Kat's husband was serious about moving to San Francisco and continued challenging her hesitations. "Before you say no, just promise me you'll apply to one job," he said. Reluctantly, she agreed. To her surprise, she landed the position—an incredible opportunity that ultimately led to their move.

While most of their friends and family supported their decision, some voiced concerns. "It's so expensive out there. How will you afford to live?" "You're 29. Will you be able to start a family while living so far away? And if you do, it will be hard... how will you manage?" Despite these doubts, they moved forward with their plans.

Initially, they thought the move would be temporary—just a couple of years before returning home. However, after settling in, their feelings quickly changed. They became captivated by the city's charm and its surrounding nature. The people inspired them, fearlessly chasing their dreams and forging their own paths. The mindset was different, opening their eyes to the many possibilities life could offer. They filled their weekends with outdoor adventures, something Kat had always longed for but hadn't been able to experience in the Midwest.

The Bay Area completely captured their hearts. Even when they took a sabbatical to travel the world, they still wanted to return to San Francisco—it had become home. Looking back, Kat is so grateful that she and her husband pushed past their comfort zones and took the risk of moving. She can hardly imagine what life might have been like if they hadn't said "yes" to something new and different. The experience showed them the power of taking a big risk—and having it pay off tenfold.

While Ren was in the Bay Area, she also became close with a coworker, Charlotte James—though her friends called her CJ. Like Kat, CJ was from the Midwest and had fascinating stories about her own experiences with moving. Her first big move was leaving her hometown, where the past four generations of her family had lived, but eventually, she had a gut feeling that there was more out there for her.

Back in the Midwest, CJ and her husband had just built a home close to her family, but they were beginning to question the life they had committed to. A snowpocalypse had just hit the city, shutting everything down. Snowed in, they began to reflect on their lives and asked themselves an important question: "Is this what we really want?" Over the past year, they had traveled to California several times and had grown accustomed to living like the locals, which made them question whether the life they had chosen was truly the right fit.

While reflecting on their life, CJ asked her husband, "What if we try to sell our house and move to California?" He wasn't hard to convince, but her family was shocked. For decades, everyone in her family had settled in the Chicago suburbs within a 20-mile radius of one another. Her great-grandparents, grandparents, parents, siblings, aunts, uncles, and cousins all lived close by. Every holiday or birthday was a family affair, and they constantly spent time together. Selling their home and moving to the West Coast went against everything the past four generations of her family had done. But something inside her told her to go, so they followed their instincts and moved.

It took only a month to sell their house, which was unprecedented in the dead of winter. In the blink of an eye, they were packing up the home they had thought they'd raise their future kids in and moving across the country. Their jobs allowed them to work remotely and transfer to West Coast offices, and they found a quaint rental home in downtown Napa Valley. CJ worked in the wine industry, and the friends they met were winemakers who owned their own vineyards. Life was picturesque, reinforcing that they had made the right decision to move.

After CJ and her husband relocated, her parents began questioning their own life choices. They had always been interested in moving somewhere else but had dismissed the idea because they wanted to stay close to their kids and future grandkids, whom they assumed would be in Chicago. No one else in the family had ever moved away, so in a way, they felt their path was predetermined, with no other option but to stay. However, a few years after CJ moved, her parents followed their dream and relocated to Colorado, with her sister following suit. Now, they are all incredibly happy they decided to take the leap and move as well.

While CJ was happy she had moved to California, the storybook life she had built eventually began to crumble. She divorced her husband due to several issues and relocated to Oakland. Her life felt completely shattered; she was alone in an unfamiliar place, sleeping on an air mattress in an empty apartment with no furniture. Through tears, she thought to herself, Will it always be this hard? Will I always be alone? I had everything... What am I doing?

At that moment, CJ realized that starting over in a new place isn't always a fairytale. There are deeply emotional and uncomfortable moments that feel overwhelming, but they are fleeting. She understood she needed to push through those challenges to reach the happiness and incredible life experiences waiting for her on the other side.

Once CJ was happily standing firm on her own, she was overcome with the familiar feeling that there was more out there for her. She enjoyed traveling abroad and knew she wanted to live in Europe next. While everyone was skeptical of her plans, she forged ahead, figuring out her visa and handling all the logistics. She arrived in Paris and started settling into her new life. It was a hard year, and she cried often, wondering if she had made a horrible mistake. Making new friends, navigating a different country, and learning a new language wasn't easy. But eventually, she hit her stride and grew to love her new friend group and life.

By moving away, CJ developed a deep appreciation for new beginnings. The opportunity to reinvent herself, meet new people, and create the life she had always dreamed of brought so much good into her life. While uprooting everything was scary and uncomfortable, the personal growth and new experiences were well worth it. Each move and new place offered its own unique lessons and memories that she'll carry with her forever. While she's enjoying living in Paris today, she's also excited to see where she'll land next and what new adventures lie ahead.

A common thread throughout Ren and her friends' experiences was that moving can be incredibly hard—it was one of the most bittersweet things they had ever done. Uprooting their lives brought discomfort, stress, and moments of doubt, making them question whether they had made the right choice. They missed out on so much back home, which caused a great deal of pain, but the rewards also brought immense joy. Many looked back on their decision to move as important turning points in their lives, opening the door to a new world of possibilities, self-discovery, and growth. In the end, most were willing to endure the hurt that comes with making a big move in exchange for the lived experiences and happiness that followed.

In summary...

• **Where you live impacts you deeply:** Your location affects your health, happiness, and overall well-being, shaping your identity, relationships, and daily life.

• **The benefits of staying close to home:** Living near family offers emotional and financial advantages, such as maintaining close relationships, sharing milestones, and accessing support for childcare and caregiving.

• **Drawbacks of staying put:** Staying in your hometown can limit personal growth, confining you to familiar routines and relationships. It may stifle curiosity, hinder exploration, and prevent you from pursuing new opportunities and reaching your full potential.

• **The importance of making an intentional decision:** Deciding whether to move requires weighing the pros and cons. It's crucial to make a deliberate decision that aligns with your personal goals, growth, and aspirations.

Thought Starters

1. How do you feel about your decision to stay put or relocate? What do you like about where you live and what feels out of alignment?

2. Where would you ideally like to live and why do you want to live there? How does your current life compare to where you want to be?

3. What's one thing you can do to get closer to where you want to live? And if you can't move, how can you make your current circumstances more ideal?

CHAPTER SIX

NO CONTACT

"The bond that links your true family is not one of blood, but of respect and joy in each other's life."
-Richard Bach

Growing up, Ren dealt with Mallory at school and then came home to a house heavily influenced by her father. It was as if he had anger simmering just beneath the surface, ready to spill over at the slightest provocation. His frustration wasn't necessarily directed at her—but it radiated outward, like ripples in a pond, affecting everything and everyone around him.

Ren would often seek refuge in her mother's warm, soothing presence, where she felt safe and loved. But with her dad, it was different. Ren could never pinpoint why, but something about him made her want to close off and shrink away. His energy was dark, filled with unresolved anger that seemed to hang in the air like smoke, suffocating her and causing her to retreat.

During family outings, he was always visibly unhappy—sighing, huffing, and puffing. It felt like Ren and her siblings were an inconvenience, keeping him from pursuing his true passions in life, like tennis. Eventually, because his presence caused more negativity and harm than good, her mom told him he didn't need to join their outings anymore, which he gladly accepted. It was a relief for everyone, as the outings became much more enjoyable without him.

As she grew older, Ren started to wonder what had happened to her father—what had shaped him into the man he was. Was he always this way? Had something broken inside him, or had life simply worn him down? Sometimes, she would tell him about her accomplishments or try to make him laugh, but he wouldn't seize the opportunity to connect. It was as if he was emotionally unavailable, unable to connect with the world in the way Ren and others longed for.

Ren naturally distanced herself from him in order to protect herself from his negativity, and others eventually followed suit. Her mom told him she wanted a divorce, and the people closest to him began to set their own boundaries because he was draining the people around him. Everyone was doing their best to be happy in their own lives, but since he carried a storm cloud over his head, he would dampen everyone's spirits if he entered their orbit.

No one could change him, and they couldn't keep wasting energy trying to brighten his world. So, the only option left was for everyone to protect themselves and choose not to be weighed down by him or allow his anger to shape their world. Some set stricter boundaries with him, while others cut off communication entirely, going no-contact.

Family significantly influences our lives because it's the first group we interact with and learn from. In our early years, we spend most of our time with family; we live in the same environment, consistently interact with our relatives, and have shared experiences together. As a result, these relationships shape who we become and the trajectory of our lives.

Having quality relationships with family during our formative years is incredibly important because it impacts our development and happiness as we age. Healthy relationships tend to have more positive interactions than negative ones, which make children feel safe and loved. Interacting productively with family teaches children how to regulate their emotions and act appropriately in social situations, ultimately giving them a better chance of developing happy and healthy relationships in all facets of life.

As a society, we encourage people to cultivate quality connections with their family because of the immense benefits this brings. We are taught that bonds with our relatives are the strongest and should take priority, which is emphasized by popular sayings like "family over everything" and "blood is thicker than water." As a result of these teachings, more than half of Americans have developed expectations that family should come first and be prioritized over all other relationships.

While we all probably strive to maintain great relationships with our families, doing so is easier said than done. We don't get to choose our family members; we are essentially assigned to live in close quarters with siblings and parents. While shared characteristics may increase the chances of getting along, at the end of the day, we are all unique individuals expected to peacefully coexist despite differing personalities, hopes, and ideals.

Family gets complicated when conflict is introduced. We are rarely perfectly in-tune with our family–or the people close to us–which causes conflict. Mismatched expectations and differing communication styles can prevent us from seeing eye to eye. These moments of misalignment with our family members can cause friction and lead to hurt feelings, disappointment, loneliness, or anger.

In order to resolve the conflict, we need to repair our relationships so we can move forward together in a positive manner. Having conflict isn't what causes families to crumble, the issue is when conflict is left unresolved. Therefore, the key to cultivating and maintaining quality bonds with our family is the ability to repair ruptures and realign our relationships. Conflict followed by some kind of repair teaches children to problem solve and find solutions to nurture their relationships. And the more they do it, the healthier they become overtime.

When something goes wrong, the repair process gets initiated by someone making a bid for connection. Examples of a bid include telling someone we want to talk things through, offering an apology, sharing a hug, or admitting fault and asking forgiveness. A successful repair occurs when both parties achieve closure by feeling more understood, connected, and warm toward each other. People who are able to successfully initiate and complete this repair process tend to have healthier and more stable relationships.

Conflict with family can easily take a turn for the worse if we aren't able to effectively engage in the repair process, especially because it becomes nearly impossible when dealing with family members who are emotionally immature. When a relationship needs to be repaired, these individuals tend to engage in unproductive behaviors like shaming, gaslighting, playing the victim, giving the silent treatment, or refusing to apologize. Their limited self awareness and ability to take accountability often leads to the relationship not being repaired, which keeps the relationship in a state of discontent.

Since many people believe we should prioritize our family over everything, some get stuck in a consistent cycle of stress and conflict with relatives. These expectations leave us searching for ways to fix a relationship to alleviate the stress and conflict, even when it's not likely to be successfully repaired. Often, taking the path of least resistance by brushing unresolved conflict under the rug seems like the only viable path forward.

Family Over Everything

↳ is a rule of behavior

↳ that individuals prefer to conform to on the condition that they believe...

most people in their network prioritize family over everything

most people in their network think they ought to prioritize family over everything

However, having consistent, unresolved conflict with a family member can be costly and detrimental to one's mental health over time. Repeated ruptures without repair causes those who are more in-tune with their emotions to build up walls over time. Love gets replaced by resentment and the relationship starts to deteriorate. If a family member can't effectively respond to bids to fix the relationship, those who are more emotionally mature eventually start distancing themselves, adjusting expectations for the relationship, and setting boundaries to cope with the stress.

One of the most drastic ways people cope with these difficult family members is through estrangement–ending the relationship by going "no contact" or "low contact" in order to get relief from the stress the relationship causes. When the relationship cannot be repaired, boundary-setting is a necessary strategy to protect our happiness. Since this decision can profoundly affect your life, it is often made after years of unresolved conflict and as a last resort in order to find peace. Going against everyone's expectations to prioritize family can be incredibly hard, especially since estrangement or going no contact with a family member is not the norm.

After making the difficult decision to cut off a family member, we often receive mixed reactions. Those who have faced similar circumstances tend to understand our perspective and support the choice to go no-contact. However, we also open ourselves up to criticism and even vilification from those who don't share this understanding. "Cold-hearted," "selfish," or "ungrateful" are common labels for people making this decision. Many people struggle to comprehend how someone could be so "cruel", and those who don't see our point of view often offer unsolicited advice, insisting we've made a mistake and should work to mend the relationship instead.

Although family estrangement is more common than many realize—affecting about one in four people—it remains a taboo topic. Few openly discuss their experiences for fear of being misunderstood, judged, vilified, or stigmatized. As a result, many navigate the process alone, grappling with a complex mix of emotions. While some may feel relief after stepping away from an unhealthy dynamic, they may also experience deep sadness and grief over the loss of a relationship with someone they love. At the same time, they must deal with the reactions of those who fail to understand that it is possible to love someone deeply yet still need to walk away.

When we remain silent, we feel isolated, as if we are the only ones experiencing this struggle. In reality, there are others quietly facing similar challenges. Until conversations about estrangement become more common, those affected may continue to struggle to heal or create meaningful change. That's why we need to talk about it—raising awareness and sharing stories can help those who are suffering realize that cutting ties is a valid option when a relationship does more harm than good. The hope is that by showcasing stories from those who have chosen this path, others who might be hurting can consider all options, rather than prioritizing family over everything, even when it hurts

Ren had been friends with Violet for about eight years and attended her holiday parties every year. They were close but had never really discussed their parents. When they finally did, they realized they had even more in common: both had strained relationships with their fathers. Ren barely spoke to hers, while Violet had cut ties with both her biological dad and her stepdad.

One day, Violet opened up a bit more about the difficulties surrounding her childhood. When she was about five years old, she and her mom stood outside a shopping mall in upstate New York as her mom pleaded with her dad for financial help. Violet's mom was struggling to care for her on her own. "I'm not paying child support," he said sharply. With that option off the table, her mom made one final plea: "At some point, Violet is going to want to know who her father is, and all I ask is that you tell her." They left that day, unsure if they would ever see or hear from him again.

A year later, Violet's mom met a man who would become her stepdad. He genuinely loved and supported Violet. He attended all her games, coached her, picked her up from school, and was always there when she needed him. Since her biological dad had no interest in being part of her life, she was deeply grateful to have a father figure who cared.

However, while Violet's stepdad had a good heart, he struggled with bipolar disorder and poor mental health. When he was doing well, he was wonderful, but during his lows, he became unpredictable. One day, he could be the most loving and gentle man; the next, he might be aggressive, verbally abusive, or even violent. After he and Violet's mom eventually separated, his behavior escalated, and he began stalking them. On one of his darkest days, the police arrested him after he was found armed with a weapon, intending to harm Violet and her mom. Following this incident, they worked to keep their distance from him and focused on moving forward with their lives.

By the time Violet was 15, she had grown curious about her biological father. Her mom rarely spoke about him, but Violet wanted to know more about where she came from. She had always felt out of place—taller and more athletic than anyone in her mom's family. She often wondered: Did her dad or his family look like her? Were they tall like she was? Did they share her passion for sports? The curiosity became overwhelming—she needed answers.

Determined, Violet decided to reach out to her biological father. She wrote him a letter—easily 20 pages long—highlighting her achievements in the hope that if he saw what a good kid she was, he might want a relationship with her. She described playing three instruments, being the MVP of her sports teams, earning straight A's, and her strong work ethic. She included pictures of herself and mailed the letter, not really expecting a response but figuring it was worth a shot.

It was a delicate situation because few people in his family even knew Violet existed. It took him weeks to respond, as he needed time to explain everything. He had gotten her mom pregnant when they were 17, left town, terminated his parental rights, and never mentioned her again. When he finally called, her stomach dropped as he said he wanted to meet her over dinner.

Their meeting was incredibly awkward. Violet barely made eye contact, but he expressed a desire to be in her life, so they tried to build a relationship. She visited his house every few months, spent time with him, and even attended his family's Christmas celebrations. Despite the progress, it never felt like he was genuinely interested in building a bond. He didn't acknowledge her accomplishments or congratulate her on her successes. While Violet was struggling financially to support herself, he never offered to help. Over time, the relationship faded until it became nearly nonexistent.

Eventually, Violet moved across the country to California, seeking a fresh start. She was recently engaged to her fiancé, and wedding planning was a challenge. When she thought about her wedding day, many traditions revolved around the bride's father. After much reflection, she realized she didn't want her dad involved in the day. He wouldn't walk her down the aisle, and she didn't want to share a father-daughter dance with him. She felt he didn't deserve those roles—or even to attend the wedding.

Exhausted by the relationship, Violet finally asked herself, Why am I doing this? She realized she didn't have to anymore. She reached out to him, explaining that he wouldn't be part of her next chapter. Their relationship wasn't working, and it was over. He responded, "I'll never give up," but she never heard from him again.

Meanwhile, Violet's stepdad remained in her life intermittently. However, due to the turmoil he caused and his history of violence, Violet set a clear boundary: he only had one more chance to maintain a relationship with her. Unfortunately, he had another bipolar episode, during which he verbally attacked *her and her family. That was the final straw. When Violet said goodbye, she tried to do so lovingly. She would always appreciate what they had shared—his love was a gift—but she could no longer endure the cycles of love and abuse. She hasn't spoken to him since.*

Violet has decided she will no longer have relationships with either her biological dad or her stepdad. While she can't control their actions or how they treat her, she can control their access to her life. She realized she didn't have to allow their negative energy to continue affecting her. Life is hard enough without the additional burden of the ongoing trauma from those relationships. She needed the space to process and heal, and the more boundaries she set, the more successful she became. Violet is committed to continuing what works: keeping them out of her life and she has zero regrets.

Knowing Violet's background, the struggles she endured, and everything she went on to accomplish, Ren felt deeply proud of her friend. She couldn't believe she hadn't known what Violet had been through. However, after a similar experience with her friend Olivia, Ren realized that people often carry deep-seated hurt that they rarely openly share. She and Olivia had been friendly for a while, but they knew little about each other's families. One day, Ren casually asked Olivia if she had any siblings. Olivia revealed that she had a sister but needed to cut her out of her life.

Olivia went on to tell Ren that her sister was known for drunken, hate-filled rants. She shared a glimpse of one particularly hurtful text her sister had sent her. After Olivia lost a pregnancy, her sister texted, "I hope you have nothing but miscarriages." Ren was stunned by the cruelty. Olivia explained that their relationship had been strained for years, but that message, in particular, made her rethink their connection entirely.

Growing up, they were never particularly close. While they played together as children, their bond faded over time. Olivia had tried to confide in her sister when their parents argued and even visited her at college in an effort to build a stronger relationship. But her sister remained distant, and their connection never deepened.

Things took a darker turn when Olivia's sister began struggling with alcohol addiction, leading to multiple trips to rehab. Despite these interventions, her binge drinking persisted, often resulting in venomous messages. When it came to Olivia, she criticized everything—from her appearance and character to her career and marriage. During Olivia's multiple miscarriages, the cruelty escalated, with accusations that she deserved the loss. These messages were never followed by apologies; instead, her sister would delete them, leaving Olivia to carry the emotional scars alone.

Despite everything, Olivia was the one expected to mend the relationship. Her parents urged her to reconcile, hoping they could all be together for family dinners and holidays. Friends echoed similar sentiments, saying, "But she's your sister—you'll regret it if you don't."

However, the toll on Olivia's mental health was undeniable. Her sister's hateful words chipped away at her confidence, making her question whether there was any truth to the hurtful things being said. Life would seem fine, and then, suddenly, Olivia would wake up to cruel texts that turned her world upside down. The emotional turmoil was overwhelming, and she ultimately had to prioritize her well-being by severing ties.

Eventually, Olivia welcomed a beautiful baby boy into the world. After enduring multiple miscarriages, she was overjoyed by his arrival and even attempted to reconcile with her sister. Unfortunately, her sister was a no-show at the baby shower and canceled multiple times when she was supposed to meet her nephew. Olivia sent pictures and updates, but her sister dismissed her efforts, eventually telling her to stop reaching out. Olivia had hoped things would be different this time, but instead, she was met with disappointment once again.

Now that her sister is no longer part of her life, Olivia feels as though a weight has been lifted. She is beginning to find genuine happiness. While she grieves the relationship they could have had, she knows it is better to protect herself and her son from an unhealthy dynamic than to force a connection that could be damaging. Olivia is embracing this new chapter, stepping into a future filled with more peace, and moving forward in a more positive direction.

The more conversations Ren had with her friends, the more she realized that many people had a story to tell about a problematic family member; you just had to be open to talking about it. One of her classmates, Scarlett, also had limited contact with her dad, which she only revealed after Ren had shared her own experience. Ren began to notice a troubling pattern among many of her friends: strained relationships with their fathers.

When Scarlett was about eight years old, her dad approached her aggressively, accusing her, "You love your mom more than me, don't you?" To temper his anger and avoid hurting his feelings, she told a white lie: "No, I love you both equally." But the truth was undeniable—the extraordinary bond she shared with her mom was clear, especially when compared to her strained, dysfunctional relationship with her dad.

Her mom felt like a ray of sunshine, while her dad was a dark cloud. Her mom found the positive in any situation, while her dad fixated on the negative. She was the calm in the eye of his storm. She was kind when he was spiteful, built Scarlett up after he tore her down, and offered wisdom when he acted immaturely. She was a safe space when he was anything but—so Scarlett naturally gravitated toward her mom and avoided her dad like the plague.

When Scarlett was about twelve years old and playing competitive sports, her dad would attend her games and yell obscenities from the stands. "Ref! Get off your knees, you're blowing the game!" he'd shout. One day, he stooped even lower, yelling at a girl on the opposing team to "eat another cookie," insinuating she was overweight. Scarlett was horrified by his behavior. After yet another game filled with his obnoxious yelling, she snapped and yelled back at him, "Shut the f*ck up!" Other parents nodded approvingly, relieved that someone had finally told him to be quiet. From then on, she begged her mom to drive her to games or arrange carpools with other parents so he wouldn't attend.

By her teenage years, Scarlett could barely tolerate being in her dad's presence. His negative energy was impossible to ignore and too much to bear. He would suck the air out of a room with his emotionally immature comments, outbursts, and incessant woe-is-me attitude. Tired of living with and being around him, Scarlett spent as much time away from home as possible. When she was home, she walked on eggshells and hid in her bedroom—the only place where she could find peace.

Scarlett and her dad never resolved their issues. No matter how she approached him with criticism about how he made people feel, he would throw a temper tantrum, get defensive, and play the victim. It was easier to keep him at arm's length and brush everything under the rug. He thought their conflicts magically resolved themselves without conversations, but Scarlett's resentment toward him built up over two decades.

The day Scarlett moved away for college was a huge relief. For the most part, she tried to remain cordial with him because, as his daughter, she felt obligated to stay in contact. However, living far away and not being in his presence was freeing. Though it felt horrible to admit, Scarlett preferred not having him in her daily life.

The only time she saw him was during the holidays. Scarlett dreaded going home and felt intense anxiety leading up to their visits. She would give him as much time as her mental health could handle, but he would inevitably guilt her into spending more time with him. When she left, he would complain or make snide comments to family members, saying she hardly spent any time with him. After another Christmas that ended in more stress and tears than joy, Scarlett decided to prioritize her peace and started distancing herself from him. She didn't see him again for six years.

Although Scarlett didn't see her dad in person, they exchanged surface-level pleasantries via email. Surprisingly, she enjoyed their relationship this way and even looked forward to his messages. Through email, he was more thoughtful and intentional with his words. If any of his emotionally immature antics made their way into an email, the computer felt like a protective force field that kept her from getting hurt. However, she knew it wasn't a realistic long-term solution—it was merely a bandage over a gaping wound.

Scarlett knew their relationship couldn't be repaired without him understanding why she stopped visiting, so she wrote him an email explaining her feelings. After rereading it to ensure it was clear but not too harsh, she hit send. She hoped for a response, but given how he historically handled conflict, she wasn't optimistic. Days turned into weeks, then months, then years, with no reply. His decision not to respond was the final blow, officially ending their relationship. Now, Scarlett rarely speaks to him, only seeing him at large family events.

Going low-contact with her dad was one of the hardest things Scarlett ever did. It was difficult to make sense of her feelings toward him. On the one hand, she was incredibly grateful to him for providing for her during her childhood. There were some glimmers of good in their relationship, but on the other hand, because he wasn't able to effectively manage his emotions and never worked on himself, there was also a lot of conflict, and she ultimately never felt emotionally safe around him. Unfortunately, this lack of emotional safety deeply hurt her, and the stress surrounding their relationship far outweighed the glimmers of good.

The hope for something healthy was why she tried to stick it out for so long and give him her time and energy. She'd suit up in her emotional armor, slap on a smile, and try to pretend everything was okay. She tried to heal on her own and forgive him without an apology or a resolution so she could happily exist in the same room as him for his own sake. But she couldn't do it; there was too much hurt and resentment living inside of her with no options to repair their relationship, so the only solution she found that provided her relief from the anxiety and stress was removing herself from the equation.

Going no contact and setting boundaries with family was one of the hardest things Ren and her friends did. Everyone's expectation that they should prioritize family over everything kept them tethered, trying to work things out, even though every interaction seemed to bring more stress and emotional pain. Ren's friends agreed that nothing cuts quite as deep as the hurt inflicted by family. For years, they endured chronic pain because of these relationships. However, the moment they gave themselves permission to cut ties, there was a shift. The pain began to dissipate, and slowly, they all started to feel better. The separation gave them the space to do the work—process, unpack, heal on their own without an apology, and put their broken hearts back together so they could start thriving in ways they never had before. Finally, by severing ties, they were able to put the chaos to rest in exchange for something they had all longed for: peace.

In summary...

- **Family is important but complex:** Family shapes us from an early age and positive relationships can be invaluable, but individual differences, miscommunications, and unmet expectations often lead to conflict.
- **Repair processes are crucial yet difficult:** Unresolved conflict within families can create significant stress, leading to resentment. Healthy relationships require effectively resolving conflict through productive discourse, but can be obstructed by emotionally immature behavior, leaving relationships fractured.
- **Setting boundaries for self-preservation:** Repeated, ongoing conflict can be stressful and erode mental health. Sometimes, it's necessary to distance yourself from family, even if it defies social norms that expect you to prioritize those relationships at all costs. While this decision can be difficult and often stigmatized, it can bring relief and personal growth to those who make it.

Thought Starters

1. Write about what you like and dislike about your current family dynamics.

2. In a perfect world, what do you want your relationships with your family to look like?

3. What's one thing you and your family need to do in order to make this family dynamic a reality?

CHAPTER SEVEN

WEDDING BELLS

*"We loved with a love that
was more than love."*
-Edgar Allan Poe

Ren met Lucas during her graduate program, and their connection deepened quickly. However, when graduation arrived a year later, life pulled them in opposite directions. Ren's career took her to Phoenix, while Lucas landed his dream job in Orlando. Determined to make their relationship work, they embraced the challenges of long distance, cherishing weekends spent together in cities across the country.

For three years, they built their individual careers and tried to see each other as often as possible. They went camping in the Tetons, explored Chicago's vibrant art scene, attended sporting events, and hiked breathtaking trails around Seattle. Each adventure reminded them of the bond they had formed during their time in grad school.

When Lucas secured a new job in Portland, Ren didn't hesitate to join him. Their reunion marked the beginning of a new chapter—a shared life in a city they could truly call their own. Their cozy apartment quickly became home, filled with laughter, music, and homemade meals. While they deeply loved one another, what stood out most was the genuine friendship they had cultivated. Not long after settling in, they decided to get married.

Since Ren had witnessed her parents' tension-filled marriage, she had long looked down on marriage and had no desire to get married herself. However, her relationship with Lucas changed her outlook. It was precisely because she had seen her parents' rocky relationship that she knew, without a doubt, that her connection with Lucas was special and worth committing to. They were strong on their own, but together, they were even stronger. Everything felt lighter and brighter in each other's presence.

As they began planning their wedding, they researched venues and started drafting a guest list. Ren quickly lost interest in having a large wedding for several reasons: the high cost, the extensive planning required, and the complications of navigating her strained relationship with her father. Lucas wasn't particularly interested in a big wedding either, so they decided to explore alternative options.

They ultimately chose to get married at city hall. On their wedding day, Ren wore a simple white dress, and Lucas donned his favorite tailored suit. In front of a few friends, they exchanged private vows—heartfelt words that reflected everything they had endured and the promises they were making for their future together.

The day was perfect because it was exactly what they had envisioned, and they were overjoyed to be married, with many adventures yet to come.

Getting married is an important milestone in many people's lives. When two people who genuinely love each other make a commitment in front of friends and family, it can make for an incredibly special day. Typically, weddings require a lot of thought, preparation, and coordination, resulting in a day so special that people celebrate their anniversary for years to come.

The marriage process typically includes a proposal, an engagement period, and finally, a wedding. There might be other events along the way, like engagement parties, bridal showers, and bachelor or bachelorette parties, too. These events present a unique opportunity to celebrate with your loved ones. Depending on your preferences and budget, these occasions can range from fairly modest with limited logistics to extremely lavish with extensive planning.

The process usually begins with the proposal, where one person asks their partner to marry them. Many try to make their proposals as unique and special as possible. However, with the rise of social media, there's more pressure on proposals than ever before, which can be stressful for some. Expectations around buying the ideal engagement ring, planning the perfect proposal, and organizing an engagement party can take an emotional and financial toll.

The tradition of exchanging engagement rings dates back thousands of years. Some believe it originated with the Egyptians, while others trace it back to the Romans. Regardless of its origins, a ring was placed on the "ring finger" of the left hand because it was believed that this finger was closely connected to the heart. Some argue that getting engaged was not originally a symbol of romantic love, as it is today, but rather a sign of ownership. While the meaning behind exchanging engagement rings has evolved over time, the tradition remains prevalent in society today.

Engagement rings have advanced over the years, from woven reeds and leather to more durable materials like ivory, flint, and bone, followed by metals such as copper, iron, and gold.

Diamond rings gained popularity after De Beers' "Diamonds are Forever" campaign, making them a symbol of marriage and a societal expectation. Today, diamonds account for 85-90% of the engagement ring market. Since diamond engagement rings are so prevalent and celebrated in society, opting for an alternative is often less desirable and not as socially accepted, even though other types of rings have been worn for centuries.

As for weddings, a typical wedding today in the U.S. costs about $35,000 with an average guest list of 115 people, and can cost even more in expensive markets and big cities. Generally, couples select a venue and fill it with ample flowers and decor. Brides tend to wear white, and couples often have bridal parties with coordinating outfits. Guests are usually treated to a feast with an open bar, music, and a night of dancing. The thoughtful touches and attention to detail from vendors and venues in the wedding industry often make for an incredibly special day for everyone involved.

While this is what a conventional wedding looks like in Western society today, the traditions, standards, and practices associated with weddings have evolved over time. In medieval times, the first documented wedding was a simple public announcement with a kiss, often without any decorations or special outfits. Eventually, weddings were more commonly held at churches and could only be officiated by ordained priests. Over the years, weddings varied between large, elaborate events and smaller, private affairs. The Victorian era (1820-1914) was particularly influential, marking the shift toward more personalized, colorful celebrations with elaborate flowers and decor—a tradition that continues today.

Several modern-day influences continue to shape our expectations and standards for the ideal engagement and wedding day. Movies, mass media, and social media have done an excellent job of romanticizing and reinforcing societal norms. These strong influences cause us to have expectations of what weddings should look like, leading us to believe our own special occasions should align with the norm of what is accepted by those close to us.

Having a Conventional Wedding
↳ is a rule of behavior
↳ that individuals prefer to conform to on the condition that they believe...

most people in their network have conventional weddings

most people in their network think they ought to have a conventional wedding too

There are people who have a conventional wedding and go on to say it was one of the best days of their lives. Some describe their wedding day as a rare and once-in-a-lifetime opportunity to have all their closest friends and family in the same place to celebrate their special day. Despite it being an incredibly costly event requiring extensive logistics and planning, some say the money and effort were well worth it and they'd do it all over again if they could.

While weddings can be one of the most joyous occasions in some people's lives, the unspoken pressures, expectations, and stress surrounding weddings are discussed less often. Weddings have become so elaborate that many people feel the need to hire a wedding planner to handle the logistics. Even then, more than half of people describe the wedding planning process as "stressful" and "overwhelming." With weddings being so glamorized and romanticized, many couples can be caught off guard when the reality of planning sets in, bringing more stress, conflict, and difficult conversations than they ever imagined.

Finances often play a big role in the stress of wedding planning. Many couples aren't prepared for how much a wedding can cost. Sam Dogan, a financial thought leader, recommends only spending 10% of your combined salary on your special day. For example, if you and your partner together make $120,000 a year, then you should only spend $12,000 on a wedding. However, given that the average cost of a wedding across the U.S. is $35,000, many couples struggle to meet societal expectations while staying within a lower budget. As a result, more than half of couples exceed their budget, on average, by about $7,300.

Sometimes a couple's parents or family might offer to pay for part of the wedding, which is incredibly generous, but often comes with strings attached. Conflict can arise when there are varying opinions on how the money should be spent, followed by constant input about traditions, the venue, and who should be invited. Navigating these dynamics and conversations can be difficult, especially when trying to find a balance between making people feel heard while ensuring your wedding aligns with your values and hopes.

Some families might have conflict and dysfunction even before the wedding planning process begins. There might be divorces, family members that don't get along, problematic relatives, or underlying resentment that's never been resolved which can make having everyone in the same room incredibly awkward or tense. While some people are willing to navigate these complexities when planning a wedding, some want to avoid the headache of having their entire family under one roof altogether.

There is no doubt that getting married should be special and celebrated. But what if you don't want to follow the norm? What if you don't want a wedding at all? What if you want a wedding that looks different from the status quo? It can be hard to go against the grain and risk disappointing loved ones who might have expectations about what your wedding should be like. However, it's important to push past the fear of disappointing others and ask yourself what you and your partner want, instead. If what you want aligns with conventional weddings, make it a reality. But if it doesn't, make sure you give yourself space from everyone else's opinions and expectations to tap into what you truly want. Resist the expectations and pressures from friends, family, the wedding industry, and society to ensure your wedding is how you want it.

Ren and Lucas had become the type of people who liked to think outside the box, but they hadn't realized how much their decision to marry at city hall would set them apart. In their world, weddings were often big, beautiful, and brimming with love. So when they opted for a simple city hall ceremony with only a few friends in attendance, they felt both excited and a little apprehensive. While their friends and family were initially surprised, everyone eventually came around with support. As word spread, some became intrigued by their choice, and one evening, Joy, Ren's best friend, texted excitedly, "We've decided to get married at city hall too—no fuss, no stress, just love."

Joy went ahead with her city hall wedding but faced unexpected backlash from her extended family, who stopped speaking to her. She and her fiancé opted for a small, intimate ceremony, inviting only immediate family, which meant not being able to invite her aunt and cousins, whom she was extremely close with. Hurt and angry, they cut off all communication, rejecting all of Joy's attempts to reconcile. Eventually, they unfollowed her on social media, and they haven't spoken in two years.

Joy wanted a smaller wedding after she learned firsthand how easy it is for a wedding to turn into a party that has nothing to do with you. During her previous engagement to her former fiancé, she constantly worried about pleasing everyone—was the venue good enough? Would people be upset if they weren't included? Family and friends felt entitled to a say, and the planning became more about meeting their desires than her own. To appease them, she and her fiancé at the time booked an expensive venue they couldn't afford because her mother-in-law preferred it and expanded the guest list to include distant relatives they barely knew.

The wedding wasn't what Joy wanted at all, and throughout the process, red flags in her relationship became impossible to ignore. She knew she needed to call off the wedding but was initially too scared of disappointing everyone. Deposits had been paid, her bridesmaids had purchased their dresses, and her bridal shower was already planned. Though afraid of disappointing others, she eventually mustered up the courage to call it off. That decision taught her a valuable lesson: when she got married, her wedding would reflect what she and her future husband wanted, not what others expected.

Eventually, she met her future husband, and they decided to get married. To keep the wedding small, they limited the guest list to immediate family. Joy struggled with not being able to include her aunt and cousins–who felt like a second family to her. She and her fiancé knew some people would be disappointed, but they hoped their loved ones would ultimately understand and support their decision. While they faced some guilt trips, passive-aggressive comments, and pressure from a few relatives, most eventually accepted their choice.

However, Joy's aunt and cousins reacted differently. Despite sending them a heartfelt message explaining her decision and reassuring them of her love, her aunt replied coldly and began speaking negatively about her to the rest of the family. The stress and guilt of knowing that people she loved were upset enough to cut ties was emotionally taxing. Joy made several attempts over the following months to repair the relationship, but her messages were met with silence–they wanted nothing to do with her.

Moving forward with the wedding was challenging, but she and her fiancé trusted their initial decision and went ahead as planned. They got married on a balcony overlooking San Francisco City Hall, with their two Great Danes and closest family members in attendance. That evening, they celebrated with an intimate dinner at a local restaurant, enjoying great food and meaningful moments with their guests. It was the best day of their lives because they had stayed true to their vision of having the smaller wedding of their dreams.

Joy still has strong relationships with nearly everyone who wasn't invited to the wedding, except for her aunt and cousins. While it saddens her that they are no longer part of her life, she has accepted it. She's proud of having stood up for what she wanted and that she didn't cave under the pressure like she used to. She's proud to have set boundaries with people she loves and that most of her relationships didn't crumble. Everything worked out as it was supposed to, and she's incredibly happy that the people who genuinely support, love, and want the best for her are still by her side as she walks into her next chapter of life.

Ren wasn't invited to Joy's wedding either, but it genuinely didn't bother her. She was happy for her friend and proud that she had done exactly what she wanted for her special day. Soon, others in Ren's life began making similar choices. Bridget, one of Lucas's old colleagues, also got married in an unexpected way, much like Joy.

Ren was scrolling through social media when she stopped in her tracks—Bridget had eloped on a mountaintop. Wearing a flowy white gown, she and her partner exchanged vows against a backdrop of rugged peaks and an endless sky. Ren beamed with joy, knowing it must have been exactly what Bridget had envisioned.

It was refreshing to see Bridget so happy, especially since Ren and Lucas knew about her previous marriage, which hadn't gone as planned. On that wedding day, Bridget had a panic attack just minutes before walking down the aisle. "Are you okay?" her sister and best friend asked, concerned. Her sister had to undo the back of her dress to help her breathe. "I'm just nervous," Bridget reassured them. In hindsight, she realized she had felt uneasy because she was walking into a wedding that was nothing like what she had envisioned for herself.

She had always dreamed of an outdoor wedding. However, after getting engaged, her fiancé's family became more involved in the wedding planning process than she had anticipated. Wedding discussions often took place during family dinners, where it became clear that there were strong expectations the ceremony would be in a Catholic church. Reluctantly, she gave up her dream of an outdoor wedding and agreed to the church ceremony her fiancé and his family wanted. She convinced herself it wasn't a big deal and that she was being a "good wife" because marriage is about compromise and sacrifice.

On her wedding day, she managed to pull herself together enough to walk down the aisle. Once the wedding was behind them, she and her husband got along reasonably well. However, she began to notice a troubling pattern: she was constantly sacrificing who she was and what she wanted to keep the peace. He valued stability, consistency, planning, and tradition—traits that were the complete opposite of her free-spirited nature.

While he appreciated her when she conformed to his way of life, she couldn't shake the feeling that he didn't truly love her for who she was at her core. To him, she was always "too much"—too spontaneous, too ambitious, and always chasing too many dreams. The compromises she made during the wedding planning process, burying her true desires, was foreshadowing of what would ultimately lead to their demise. After several years together, they filed for divorce.

She struggled to process her feelings about the relationship in the moment. She tended to go through the motions, never pausing to reflect on how she was living. By not checking in with herself, her true feelings about her marriage caught her off guard. The biggest lesson she took away from that relationship was the importance of regularly checking in with herself—assessing her feelings and ensuring she was heading in the direction she truly wanted.

Eventually, she met someone new. His name was John, and he changed everything for her. Her relationship with John felt right—

they were in sync, and their views on life aligned. He was more of a free spirit and wasn't afraid to challenge tradition and social norms. They dated for only a year before getting engaged, but it's true what they say: when you know, you know. And she most definitely knew.

This time, Bridget carefully considered what she truly wanted for her wedding. Together, she and John decided to elope and get married on a mountaintop. There were many reasons for this choice. Financially, they didn't want to go into debt over a party that didn't hold much meaning for them. The restrictions due to the coronavirus outbreak would have forced them to wait too long to marry safely. They also weren't interested in dedicating their free time outside of work to planning a wedding. Most importantly, they wanted the experience to feel intimate and personal.

On their wedding day, they got ready together and drove out to the mountain range in Colorado. They hiked with a photographer to the summit and had a truly special ceremony, exchanging deeply personal vows. While it was bittersweet not having their family and friends there, they made an effort to include them by sending personal cards and FaceTiming them on their special day.

They anticipated mixed reactions from their family and friends, ranging from genuine support to disappointment. However, they didn't expect their decision to elope would lead to a year-long divide with a family member. Bridget's sister-in-law felt entitled to attend the ceremony and disapproved of their decision, which strained their relationship. Although they eventually mended the rift and are now on better terms, their connection hasn't fully returned to what it once was.

Knowing everything that happened leading up to and after their wedding, they would still make the same decision. It was a tough choice, but their wedding ended up being a powerful opportunity for John and Bridget to do what they wanted. They could have caved at the first sign of pressure, but instead, they stood firm in what was right for them. Standing on that mountaintop, being their most authentic selves, remains one of the best decisions they've ever made.

Over the next couple of years, Ren attended several weddings of friends who truly wanted more traditional ceremonies, each one incredibly special. While she loved when couples chose unique ways to celebrate, she couldn't deny that there was something magical about reuniting with all her friends at a big, beautiful wedding. Shedding tears alongside the couple's loved ones, witnessing their love on full display, was always an unforgettable experience.

It had been a while since one of Ren's friends opted for a more unconventional wedding—until Stella asked her to be a bridesmaid. Stella had always dreamed of a destination ceremony. She chose to have her dream wedding but, due to complicated family dynamics, decided not to invite her family. Instead, she surrounded herself with her closest friends for an intimate island wedding, celebrating with beach days and starry nights.

Growing up, Stella's family was complicated. Her dad left when she was about five years old. She has immense respect for her mom, who, as a single parent, provided for her and her brother after their dad left. Stella genuinely appreciates her mom's efforts in caring for them and ensuring they had everything they needed and more. However, the emotional side of their relationship caused significant hurt and pain—pain her mom has never acknowledged or taken accountability for—causing their fragile bond to crumble over the years.

Her mom often created conflict within the family. She would say something negative about Stella to her brother and then say something negative about her brother to Stella, going out of her way to stir up unnecessary tension. Family members were constantly fighting, and her mom always played the victim, claiming, "I have no idea why they're mad or why this happened," even when it was clear she had instigated the conflict. The nonstop friction within her family ultimately led Stella to sever ties with them to protect her peace.

After Stella got engaged, she knew immediately that her family wouldn't be invited to the wedding, as their presence would have made things extremely uncomfortable. She emailed them to share the news, and most responded with well wishes. Her mom expressed disappointment at not being included, which Stella understood, but she still stands by her decision.

The wedding was exactly what Stella and her husband had envisioned. They didn't let any outside noise influence their decisions and did exactly what they wanted. They spent the week with 15 of their closest friends and some family in Jamaica. It was a beautiful celebration, and everyone got along perfectly.

Many people struggle to understand or empathize with Stella's decision to cut off communication with her family and exclude them from her wedding. Those who haven't experienced a similar situation often say, "But you were always so close with your mom." However, they've never had to navigate this kind of relationship with a parent. Sometimes, a relationship can cause more harm than good, and prioritizing your own happiness becomes essential.

After the wedding, Stella's father-in-law inquired about her mom. "Are you sure you don't want to have a relationship with her?" he asked. Stella replied, "You know what, I'm good. I'm actually really good." He nodded softly and said, "Okay, I just want to make sure you aren't going to have any regrets." Her husband eased his dad's mind further, "The one thing about Stella is she's decisive. If she thought she was going to regret something, she would have already done it."

Ultimately, Stella realized that to protect her well-being, she needed to take care of herself—even if it meant being perceived as selfish. If her family had been willing to put in the effort to work on themselves, things might have turned out differently. But she is happier and more fulfilled than ever before and knows she made the right decision—for her wedding and for her life moving forward.

Ren and her friends made intentional choices for their special days, prioritizing their own vision of love and commitment over societal expectations. Despite the opinions of their loved ones, they stayed true to what felt right for them. The journey wasn't without challenges—there were moments of friction, tough conversations, and doubts—but in the end, their weddings reflected who they truly were and what they wanted for themselves. By resisting the pressure to conform, they created celebrations that felt more personalized, authentic, and meaningful than if they had simply followed the norm or what others expected of them.

In summary...

• **Weddings are a joyous time rooted in tradition:**
Weddings are often elaborate events filled with traditions,
requiring extensive planning and coordination. Though
celebrated as a once-in-a-lifetime occasion, the pressure
to fulfill others expectations can be overwhelming.

• **Various pressures can lead to conforming:** Financial
stress, family contributions with strings attached,
complex family dynamics, and societal expectations often
add to the challenges couples face during the wedding
planning process. These pressures can cause people to
conform, even if it doesn't feel right.

• **Important to prioritize personal desires:** Couples
should focus on what they truly want, whether that aligns
with a conventional wedding or not. It's essential to resist
societal pressures and embrace alternative celebrations if
desired and it aligns with personal values.

Thought Starters

1. How do you feel about the expectations surrounding conventional weddings? What aspects align with your beliefs and which parts don't?

2. If you've been married before, what was your wedding like and was the day what you wanted? And if you're not married, what do you envision for yourself in the future?

3. If you're already married, how can you support other people in making their visions a reality? And if you aren't married, what steps can you take to make sure you do what you want?

CHAPTER EIGHT

ZERO PROOF

> *"Not drinking makes me a lot happier."*
> -Naomi Campbell

At fifteen, Ren attended her first high school party. She hadn't wanted to go—her heart longed for a quiet night at home with her favorite book. But her mom insisted, worried that Ren would stop getting invited if she didn't go. Reluctantly, Ren gave in, got ready for the party, and met up with the other kids from school.

When she arrived, she downed a drink and joined in on the fun. The alcohol loosened her up and helped her talk to people she never thought she'd approach. Over time, it became her weekend routine. She'd meet her friends, drink too much, and party until the early hours of the morning.

But each morning was the same. Ren would wake up in a fog of regret, her stomach churning and her head pounding. Beneath the physical hangover was anxiety that settled like a weight in her chest. She'd replay the night in her head, picking apart every interaction, wondering if she'd embarrassed herself. *I'm never drinking again,* she often thought to herself. Yet, by the time the next weekend rolled around, she'd be back at it again, swept up by the fear of missing out and the pressure to fit in.

Years passed, and if there was a party, Ren was always there. She had countless stories—some hilarious, some cringeworthy. She met some incredible people, made memories she'd treasure forever, and developed social skills she never thought she'd have. She could hold a conversation with a stranger, navigate awkward silences, and charm her way through any situation.

But, deep down, Ren knew this life wasn't for her, and it never had been. She wasn't the girl who loved staying out until sunrise or found joy in a room full of loud music and endless drinks. She had a large group of friends who liked the social "party girl" she had morphed into, but she doubted they'd like who she truly was.

For more than a decade, Ren leaned into the party persona. Then, one morning, after another night out when she wished she had stayed home, Ren decided she was done with drinking. She couldn't keep living a life that didn't feel like hers. Her friends were skeptical at first. "Come on, just one drink," they'd say. But Ren stood her ground. She started saying no to the parties and yes to the things that truly made her happy.

Instead of hangovers, Ren woke up feeling refreshed. She replaced late-night bars with cozy dinners at home and wild nights out with quiet moments of deep reflection. She got to know herself even better, discovered new hobbies, deepened her friendships with people who supported her choices, and felt more herself than she ever had before.

Looking back, Ren didn't entirely regret her years of partying. They had taught her valuable lessons, given her unforgettable memories, and shaped her into who she was. But she was ready to embrace the person she had always been deep down—the person she had kept tucked away for far too long. Deciding to give up alcohol allowed Ren to take another step closer to becoming the person she truly was.

Drinking alcohol is deeply embedded in society, touching almost every aspect of life. Whether at a pub, concert, wedding, restaurant, sporting event, or even someone's home, alcohol is usually there. It's a popular way to socialize, ease tension, and celebrate. Alcohol has the power to turn a stuffy room into a lively gathering, transform anxiety into confidence, and make celebratory toasts more special. For many, drinking a few times a week is considered normal.

Alcohol has been around for thousands of years. By the 1800s, it was already deeply ingrained in American culture, with widespread heavy drinking. This sparked moral objections from prohibitionists, who sought to implement a strict ban. In 1919, Prohibition—a nationwide alcohol ban—was officially passed by Congress. However, it failed to stop people from drinking, ultimately leading to its repeal in 1933. Afterward, alcohol's popularity surged again, ushering in the modern era of alcohol consumption in America.

Today, about 63% of Americans drink alcohol, a figure that has remained stable since the Civil War. Drinking is widely normalized and integrated into daily life. Some people report benefits from moderate alcohol consumption, such as reduced stress and improvements in physical and mental health. Many drinkers also feel more socially connected.

However, discussions about the health risks associated with alcohol are becoming more mainstream. Despite its widespread use, these risks are often overlooked. The alcohol industry is notorious for downplaying the dangers while overemphasizing the benefits. Even moderate drinking carries well-established health risks. In the U.S., alcohol is a leading cause of premature death and has been linked to cancer and various other illnesses. It can also increase anxiety and depression.

Despite these negative consequences, public perception of alcohol remains largely positive and accepting. Drinking is so ingrained in American culture that many people expect others to drink as well. As a result, individuals may feel pressured to follow the norm, even if they don't want to, simply because those around them do and expect them to do the same.

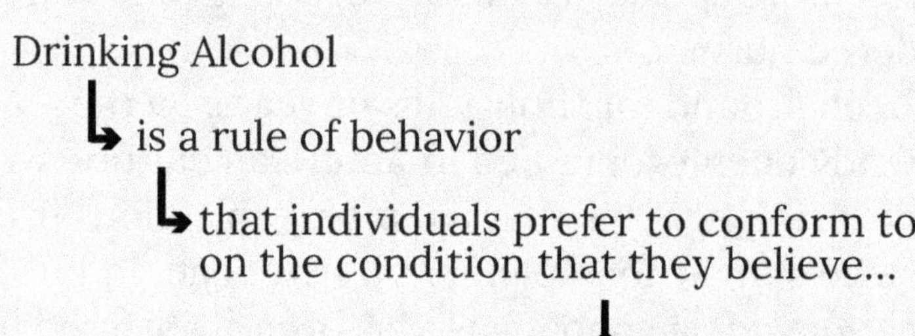

People can feel pressured to drink at any stage of life, but it typically begins in youth. Young people have a particularly strong desire to fit in, and their friends can greatly influence their decisions about drinking. Peer pressure can be direct, such as encouraging someone to drink or giving them a hard time if they don't. More subtle forms include refilling someone's drink or buying them another without asking.

When it comes to drinking, many young people mimic what they see others doing. If the popular kids at school drink, it can create the illusion that "everyone" is doing it, making others more likely to join in to feel included. Standing out as different can be difficult, so if drinking seems like the norm, many will participate just to fit in.

Getting older doesn't make people immune to peer pressure, either. Adults can still feel pressured to drink to fit in, sometimes drinking more than they want to in order to meet social expectations. Pressure can come from having drinks topped up without consent, being handed an extra round of shots, or feeling obligated to participate in celebratory toasts. While people are often encouraged to "just say no," doing so can bring unwanted attention or even lead to being excluded from future social events.

To manage this pressure while limiting their alcohol consumption, many people develop strategies. Some order non-alcoholic drinks that resemble alcoholic ones, while others drive to events so they have a "valid" excuse not to drink. Many also seek out friends who drink moderately or not at all to avoid the pressure altogether.

Millennials and Gen Z are at the forefront of questioning alcohol's role in society. With greater awareness of its health risks and mental health effects, many are choosing to drink less than previous generations. Concerns about acting out of character and having those moments captured on social media also contribute to their more cautious approach. While some are reducing alcohol consumption in favor of other substances like cannabis and psychedelics, the majority still drink.

Holly Whitaker, author of *Quit Like a Woman*, predicts that alcohol consumption may follow a path similar to tobacco use. Smoking was once widely accepted, but as awareness of its risks grew, public sentiment shifted, leading to smoking bans and health warnings on cigarette packages. Whitaker believes alcohol could undergo a similar cultural shift in the future. However, until then, those who choose not to drink remain in the minority, often navigating peer pressure and societal expectations.

Initially, Ren didn't know anyone who abstained from alcohol. The first person she encountered was Sabrina, whom she met at a networking event. After they connected on social media, Ren quickly noticed Sabrina's content about sobriety. Curious about her reasons for not drinking, Ren reached out to ask, and Sabrina was more than happy to share.

Sabrina's time in the alcohol industry led to a harsh realization—her drinking had spiraled out of control. One Monday morning, she had just finished presenting to the executive leadership team at work while still drunk from the night before. Her eyes were bloodshot and burning; all she wanted to do was to close them. She managed to get through the presentation, but afterward, her boss approached her and said she needed to cut back on her drinking. "You can't keep doing this, kiddo," he warned.

Drinking had slowly become the center of her universe. Wine was infused into every part of her life—whether at a business dinner, happy hour, conference, wine bar, at home, or at work. Balance and moderation were never her strong suits; she could never stop at just one or two glasses. When she drank, she went all out, often to the point of blacking out. Her drinking had never impacted her work before—until that presentation to senior leadership, when she was still feeling the effects of last night's drinks.

That day was a major wake-up call for Sabrina—maybe she did have a drinking problem. Soon after, she left her job in search of an industry that didn't revolve around alcohol. At the same time, she enrolled in a recovery program, where she learned about substance abuse, her triggers, and how to regulate her emotions without alcohol. Determined to examine her habits and make a change, she slowly began to envision a life without drinking—and realized that it was, in fact, possible for her.

Coming out of the recovery program, Sabrina decided to get sober. She cried for hours, wondering how she could have a fulfilling life without alcohol. Practically every advertisement portrayed life's greatest moments being celebrated with champagne. Would she ever truly enjoy New Year's again? How would she go on a date without drinking? How would she get married again without alcohol? She worried she'd have to decline invitations to maintain her sobriety or that, if she did attend, the experience would feel dull and watered down.

She stayed sober for 67 days, but her sobriety ended on New Year's Eve. That night, she decided to drink to practice moderation. Unfortunately, she drank too much and had to go home before the ball dropped. Her drinking continued for the next five months as she traveled across Europe, caught in a vicious cycle of overconsumption, blackouts, and regret.

When Sabrina returned home, her drinking persisted. Then, on a random Sunday, everything changed. She was sitting on the couch with her favorite white wine when she looked down at her glass and thought to herself: *This can't be the thing that makes you happy. This can't be it for you—there's so much more to life.* Slowly, she walked over to the sink, grabbed the unfinished bottle, and poured the rest down the drain. That random Sunday became the first day of the rest of her life.

To get sober, Sabrina occasionally attended AA meetings, read "quit lit," listened to sobriety podcasts, and experimented with mocktails. For the first year, she experienced what's known as the "pink cloud"—the honeymoon phase of recovery, where life seemed lighter and brighter, and she felt euphoric from not drinking.

However, the most influential factors in her sobriety were committing to therapy and getting her dog, Mazzie—both of which significantly improved her life and helped her embrace sobriety more happily.

Now, Sabrina has been sober for three and a half years. Thinking about her alcohol-free life makes her emotional. She feels like the best version of herself—realizing she is enough, just as she is. She no longer needs alcohol to make her funnier, prettier, or more outgoing. She moves through life with more optimism, confidence, and a sense of peace she never thought possible. Becoming sober is one of her greatest accomplishments, and she can't wait to see all the wonderful things she will achieve in this next chapter of her life.

Seeing Sabrina thrive without alcohol intrigued Ren, but at the time, she never seriously considered following suit. She didn't necessarily have a drinking problem—she just didn't enjoy the aftermath of overindulging. However, a couple of years later, she reunited with Ellie, an old friend from grad school who had also started to limit her drinking. While attending their classmate's wedding in Wisconsin, Ellie hesitantly shared her plan to have only a couple of drinks so she could enjoy a hangover-free weekend.

It was mid-morning the day before the wedding, and their friend group met up at a dive bar for breakfast. One of their classmates thought it would be fun to have the bartender bring over a round of shots for the entire group. Everyone grabbed their shot, said cheers, clinked their glasses together, tapped them on the table, and threw them back. Ellie, however, lifted her shot to her lips, pretended to take it, then quickly set it back down, hiding it behind a beer bottle on the table.

Suddenly, chants erupted from twenty of Ellie's grad school friends, filling the tiny dive bar: "Ellie! Ellie! Ellie!" Someone had noticed she hadn't taken her shot and rallied the group to pressure her into drinking it. Back in grad school, Ellie used to drink a lot to fit in, but now she rarely did. She was tired of the hangover-induced anxiety that lingered long after a night out, and she had come to realize that living without hangovers was far better than the short-lived fun of drinking.

As her friends chanted her name, Ellie felt the weight of everyone's eyes on her, urging her to take the shot. Her cheeks and neck flushed red with embarrassment, and she could feel the pressure mounting as their voices grew louder. She had no idea how she was going to get out of it. She had two choices: give in or stay true to herself and say no.

As the chanting continued, Ellie was tempted to take the shot just to make it stop. But she had promised herself before the weekend: no shots, only a couple of drinks. Ultimately, she chose to stand her ground. As nicely as possible, she told her friends she wasn't going to do it. They kept chanting, convinced she would cave. Holding firm, she said, "You can stand there and chant all day—I'm not taking the shot." The chanting awkwardly faded as they realized she was serious, and the group eventually eased back into their conversations.

While Ellie was proud of herself for staying true to her decision, she couldn't shake the worry about what her friends thought. They must think I'm a loser, she thought. Then, she felt a tap on her shoulder. Expecting her classmate to tease her, she turned around—but was met with his unexpected support. "That was powerful. You had a room full of people pressuring you, and you stayed strong. That was way cooler than taking the shot." Ellie's eyes welled with tears, grateful for his reassurance in that moment. Ren, watching it all unfold from across the bar, was deeply impressed by Ellie's ability to resist such blatant, palpable peer pressure.

About four months later, Ellie decided to give up alcohol for good. It wasn't difficult for her—she had never truly enjoyed drinking anyway. When she did drink, she often went overboard, regretting it the next day. Her weekends became a cycle of drinking too much, nursing a hangover in a puddle of anxious despair, and repeating it all over again.

The hardest part about quitting wasn't giving up alcohol—it was worrying about what others would think. Drinking had helped her fit in, and now she felt like an outsider. When out with friends, she would try to arrive early to order a non-alcoholic beer or cocktail, hoping to pass it off as the "real" thing. She dreaded ordering water or a mocktail at business dinners, knowing everyone at the table would overhear. People speculated that she might be pregnant, and some even made insensitive jokes about her choice not to drink.

Despite these challenges, Ellie stuck to her decision. She ordered what she wanted—not what others expected. Looking back, she feels silly for ever caring about what people thought. Now, after two and a half years without alcohol, she wouldn't trade this life for anything. She feels better physically and mentally, and she wakes up happy every day instead of riddled with anxiety. She has transformed from a self-conscious girl who drank to fit in into someone confident and proud of her alcohol-free life. She is more herself than ever before and feels at peace with her decision—so much so that she doesn't think she'll ever go back.

While Ren was deeply impressed by Ellie's ability to withstand peer pressure and celebrated her decision to not drink, she continued drinking as usual until she attended a networking event and felt like she had embarrassed herself. She woke up the next day with her usual feelings of anxiety and regret, but this day was different—she was finally fed up.

About a year after Ren stopped drinking, she was catching up with Bri, an old friend. They had met years earlier at a booze-filled bachelorette party in Scottsdale and had only hung out at events where everyone was drinking. Ren shared that she no longer drank, to which Bri responded, "Funny you say that... I've recently decided to cut out alcohol, too."

Bri shared how hard it was as the only person in her friend group who didn't drink. Being a little tipsy made her social and fun, allowing her to fit in with everyone. But when she stopped drinking, she stopped fitting in and suddenly felt different from all of her friends—she struggled to feel like she was enough. She worried they'd think she was quiet and boring, someone who wasn't any fun. Either she was the friend who stayed home or the friend who came out but didn't drink; it seemed like a lose-lose situation.

Bri never drank that much to begin with, but during the COVID pandemic, she drank a lot more than usual. Since most businesses were closed and there were very few options for activities, Bri and her roommate started drinking a lot of wine at home. Eventually, she noticed the drinking was impacting her health, so she cut it out to see if it helped her feel better. After two months of not drinking, Bri opened a bottle of her favorite wine and didn't even like the taste of it anymore. From then on, she cut back significantly and only drank on occasion if she really wanted to.

It's been hard being the only one in her friend group not drinking. She remembers thinking that it would be so much easier if she just drank like everyone else. She had so much guilt. Why couldn't she just be like other people her age? Why couldn't she just want to drink? Why did she have to care so much about not drinking? But the reality was, drinking wasn't working for her, and it didn't feel worth it anymore. Her health and feeling her best were so much more important than having a drink.

Dealing with pressure from others was tough for Bri. If she stayed in, friends would guilt her with, "Come out, we never see you!" When she did go out, it was hard not to drink when everyone else was enjoying their alcoholic beverages. Excuses like Dry January or an early workday were all valid reasons no one questioned, but saying no for her health or better sleep often led to pushback—"Just have one, Bri!" When Bri shared her reasons for not drinking, some would get defensive, assuming she was judging them when she was simply explaining her choice.

Now, Bri turns down alcohol 90-95% of the time, and while it's had countless benefits, the hardest part was handling others' reactions to her not drinking. Relationships with people who pressured her or reacted defensively fizzled out. But with that loss came a lot of gain—the people who are still in Bri's life are the ones who value her, support her, and celebrate her when she doesn't drink. The social pressure gradually lessened over time, and now it's much easier for Bri to stay true to herself by not going out or drinking as much, no matter what people think of her.

Ren and her friends each made the personal decision to either stop drinking entirely or significantly reduce their alcohol consumption. This choice came with its challenges. They had to *navigate social circles where drinking was the norm, manage the discomfort of explaining and justifying their choices to friends and family, and endure both subtle and not-so-subtle pressure to conform. At times, they grappled with the fear of being judged or feeling as though they no longer belonged. Yet, over time, they learned how to navigate these hurdles with growing confidence, eventually standing firm in their choices and fully embracing their alcohol-free lives.*

In summary...

- **Alcohol is deeply ingrained in American society:** Drinking is considered the norm. Its presence at weddings, sporting events, and other gatherings normalizes alcohol consumption and establishes social expectations. While moderate consumption is widely accepted, abstaining is far less common.
- **Being pressured to drink can happen at any age:** Peer pressure influences drinking behaviors from adolescence through adulthood. This pressure often stems from drinking being a normalized pastime that brings people together. Strategies to manage this include setting personal boundaries and finding social circles that respect the choice not to drink.
- **The Importance of rethinking our alcohol consumption:** Younger generations, such as Millennials and Gen Z, are increasingly questioning the role of alcohol in their lives. Concerns about health, mental well-being, and public perception (e.g., behaviors ending up on social media) have led many to reduce consumption or explore alternatives like cannabis or psychedelics.

Thought Starters

1. What's your current relationship with alcohol? How does this relationship and your drinking habits align with the standards of today, and how does it differ?

2. What role would you like alcohol to have in your life? How does your current life compare to this goal?

3. What's one action you can take in order to make your ideal relationship with alcohol a reality?

CHAPTER NINE

THE AMERICAN DREAM

"The American Dream is a phrase that we'll have to wrestle with all of our lives. It means a lot of things to different people. I think we're redefining it now."

-Rita Dove

From the outside looking in, Ren's childhood seemed picture-perfect. She lived in one of the largest houses on the block in a beautiful suburb, attended gymnastics and piano lessons, and played various sports throughout the year. Every few years, her family traveled to exciting new destinations for vacations. Her parents worked tirelessly to achieve "the American Dream," and by all appearances, they had succeeded.

On paper, they had the dream life, but the reality within that house felt cold and hollow. Ren's family was often scattered, tucked away in different corners of the house, living their separate lives. When everyone came together, they pushed each other's buttons, sometimes purposely, often leading to fighting, tension, and miscommunication. Conflicts were never properly addressed; instead, they were swept under the rug, causing everyone to retreat back into their own worlds, leaving walls—both literal and figurative—between them.

Since Ren was dealing with Mallory at school, she embraced the separation from her family at home, unable to bear any more conflict or stress. While Ren was incredibly grateful for everything she had materially, as she grew older, she realized that something crucial was missing from her childhood: a tight-knit family with a deeper emotional bond.

Even family vacations, which should have brought them closer together, felt disjointed. Although they traveled to incredible destinations, strained relationships, her father's negative energy, stressful travel logistics, and living in close quarters only created more conflict. They posed for family photos with forced smiles, but apart from her special bond with her mom, there were few heart-to-heart conversations or moments of shared laughter. Occasionally, a flicker of connection would surface, only to be quickly extinguished by yet another argument.

After returning from these trips, they would fall back into their usual routines. As Ren grew older, she began to see the stark difference between a house full of things and a home full of love. Despite having all the material possessions in the world, they didn't bring her happiness. What she truly longed for was a peaceful life filled with deeper, harmonious relationships.

While Ren remained grateful for the comforts she had growing up, she knew she wanted a different life for herself. She started consciously prioritizing her relationships, and the returns she experienced were immeasurable. She didn't own a fancy home or car, but her life with Lucas and a small circle of friends was simple, peaceful, and filled with joy. It was then she realized she was living the American Dream—it just looked much different than what others might have expected.

The American Dream is a concept that inspires many people to work towards creating a better life for themselves. The premise is that everyone has the right and freedom to achieve prosperity and happiness, regardless of where they were born or the circumstances they were born into.

The idea was popularized by historian James Truslow Adams in 1931 during the Great Depression. Adams was drawn to the idea of the American Dream because he felt the country had strayed from its original ideals by idealizing wealth and economic prosperity above all else. He argued that the American Dream was actually a "dream of a better, richer, and happier life for all."

However, the meaning of the American Dream slowly transformed from what Adams had envisioned into the very thing he critiqued. It shifted from an inspiring message of solidarity and equality to one focused on consumerism and chasing material wealth with an individualistic, every-person-for-themselves mentality.

Several pivotal moments in history helped shape the essence of the American Dream. Homeownership became a foundational element, for example. In the 1950s, many people moved to the suburbs after the war to live "the good life." Having a home in suburban neighborhoods for their picture-perfect nuclear family became the standard. Over the years, the importance of homeownership was reinforced in society to the point that it became a psychological necessity and a symbol of independence, financial freedom, and the American Dream.

After the war, there was also a rise in the American Dream being associated with consumer goods. With all the new technology and products created to make life at home easier, people started filling their homes with "more, new, and better" household items. People began buying the newest appliances and products, which caused many to feel pressure to conform and keep up with their neighbors. Our fascination with material goods has continued to grow over time, with many believing the "good life" depends on the things you own.

Education became an essential pathway to securing a good-paying job, which is considered the gateway to the American Dream. Access to education is key to upward mobility for many and ensures U.S. citizens have opportunities to pursue their dreams. In the 2000s, companies started adding degree requirements to job postings that didn't previously require degrees, setting the standard that education was essential to securing good-paying jobs.

Now, there is often a standard path people are expected to take to achieve the American Dream. We need to work hard to obtain an education and get a respectable job. In our personal lives, we're supposed to get married, buy a home, and have kids—in that exact order. Then, we work hard for years to provide for our family, pay off our mortgage, and save for retirement. That way, when we retire around 60, we can spend our time doing what we want.

But what if you don't want to walk this path and prioritize these milestones? What if your idea of the American Dream looks different from what society has outlined for us? It can be challenging to do things differently when everyone expects you to follow the standardized path.

Chasing the American Dream
↳ is a rule of behavior
↳ that individuals prefer to conform to on the condition that they believe...

| most people in their network chase the American Dream | most people in their network think they ought to chase the American Dream too |

While chasing the American Dream can be beneficial, motivating, and fulfilling for many, its central tenets sometimes might not align with what you value and how you want to live your life. Younger generations are starting to forge a new path with an updated outlook on what the American Dream means.

Young people are embracing lifestyles focused on happiness and life experiences instead of accumulating material goods. Some have started to question the value of a college education that results in massive debt, favoring alternative avenues. There are significant barriers keeping them from homeownership, so many are embracing the perks of renting, while others have bought into the dream and now have buyers' remorse due to undesirable locations, hidden costs, high interest rates, or feeling tied down. Instead of embracing hustle culture, vying for good-paying jobs, and climbing the corporate ladder, some are more interested in flexible mid-level jobs that allow for more time to experience life.

Younger generations aren't favoring just any life experiences; instead, they are prioritizing new ones. Novel experiences are important because they grab our attention and slow time down, while monotony speeds time up. If you fill your life with monotonous experiences, life will feel short and watered down. Meanwhile, if you're constantly exploring unfamiliar places, the hours stretch out, and you'll feel as if you've lived ten lives in one day, thanks to a concept called the oddball effect. That's why young people are spending their money on travel—by exposing themselves to novel situations, they are forced to pay more attention, which expands their life and makes their days feel longer, distinct, and more fulfilling.

While the American Dream we all know is still prevalent today, people are starting to realize they have autonomy and the ability to choose something different for themselves. It starts with understanding what's important to you, questioning which aspects of the American Dream are relevant to your own life, and creating a new vision of the American Dream you want for yourself.

Ren had learned that the conventional ideals of the American Dream didn't always lead to happiness, so she chose to explore an alternative path. She now prioritizes her relationships, works flexible jobs instead of climbing the corporate ladder, and happily rents small apartments that let her move and experience new cities. One of her grad school friends was living similarly—but only after experiencing firsthand the cost of sacrificing personal happiness for a career.

On the morning Beth was let go from her job, she woke up earlier than usual with a gut feeling that she needed to check her phone. A random 15-minute meeting had been added to her calendar first thing in the morning with HR. She joined the video call, and they delivered the unfortunate news: "Unfortunately, today is your last day working here." Beth immediately burst into tears and could feel her heart break. After nine months in her dream job, she was let go as if her hard work and sacrifices meant nothing to them.

For much of her life, Beth lived to work. She hoped one day she'd have more time to experience the world beyond her career. However, with the way she prioritized work, it felt like she'd have to wait until retirement to finally get there. She told herself she'd have more time after finishing her undergraduate degree, but then she went to grad school. After grad school, she thought she'd have time, but she got her first job and focused on climbing the corporate ladder. With each accomplishment and milestone, a new *goalpost appeared, creating a never-ending cycle of chasing the future and never fully experiencing the present.*

The day she was let go from her job changed her outlook forever. From that point on, she started working the hours specified in her contract instead of going above and beyond for companies that could lay her off at a moment's notice. She began taking her paid time off and using it to travel the world. Over two years, she visited ten new countries and accumulated what feels like a lifetime of memories. This experience was a wake-up call, reminding Beth that work is merely a means to make money so we can make the most of our time outside of work.

Now, she chases experiences rather than material goods or career milestones. She and her husband have intentionally not jumped into homeownership because it's cheaper for them to rent. They don't worry about home repairs or maintenance and have the freedom to easily move to a new neighborhood or state if they want. They share a car they've had for ten years; the air conditioning is broken, and the speakers don't work, but they don't have a car payment, and it gets them from point A to point B perfectly. As a result of not having a more expensive mortgage or a car payment, they've funneled all of their excess money into the stock market, which has grown their net worth significantly.

Once they stopped chasing the so-called American Dream or worrying about trying to obtain the things everyone else has, they realized they're actually living their American Dream right now. They don't own a home or a fancy car, but they don't have any debt, and their net worth is growing substantially year over year. They have the financial freedom to travel the world and invest in memorable experiences, which make them feel fulfilled. They have their health and mobility, and most importantly, they have time, which they believe is the most valuable resource of all and the cornerstone of their American Dream.

While Ren had a lot in common with Beth, she met others along the way who also forged their own paths in ways she'd never considered or imagined before. She met Emma, and they hit it off instantly due to their shared interests. Ren was always impressed by Emma's career—she had landed an amazing, well-paying job at a flashy start-up that was eventually acquired. Emma's success inspired Ren to aim higher, and she hoped that one day, she too would find her footing the way Emma had.

However, Emma and her husband had always wanted to travel far and wide, but with the world practically shut down due to the COVID pandemic, those dreams kept getting pushed farther and farther into the future. One day, while reflecting on their lives and how they were spending their time, they couldn't help but wonder: What are we doing with our lives? They worked a lot, but they didn't feel fulfilled and knew there was more to life than their living room.

The first two years of the pandemic seemed to fly by due to the monotony, and suddenly, they were 33 years old. The pressure to settle down, buy a house, and have kids kept creeping into their minds. But what about their dream of traveling the world? When would they get to do that? They realized they wouldn't be able to accomplish it by just taking their paid time off from work and going on sporadic trips, so they decided to take a risk by quitting their jobs and traveling the world for 18 months. Of course, they recognized how privileged and fortunate they were to have been able to do this—very few people could comfortably make the same choice, and they were immensely grateful for the opportunity.

Quitting their jobs and giving up their steady flow of income was terrifying. Emma had been taught to go to college, get a good-paying job, save her money, buy a house, pay off her mortgage, and continue saving so that she could retire in her sixties. Once she retired, she would finally get to travel and enjoy her time. So, quitting her good-paying job and spending some of their savings on travel—which could've been used as a down payment for a house—was counter to everything she had been taught.

Regardless, Emma and her husband handed in their resignations and told their families about their plans. While people were generally supportive, some were skeptical and doubtful of their decision. What they were doing was so different from what anyone in their family had done before. A lot of their relatives couldn't wrap their heads around why anyone would do this. But they were certain that traveling the world was what they wanted to do, so they got to work planning their trip.

They began their adventures in South Africa and concluded their journey in the Patagonian mountains of Chile, where Ren and Lucas joined them to celebrate the end of their trip. Over 18 months, they traveled to 24 countries—going on a safari in South Africa, trekking with gorillas and volunteering at a school in Uganda, skiing in Japan, marveling at the Taj Mahal in India and the pyramids in Egypt, driving across New Zealand in a camper van, and unwinding at the Blue Lagoon in Iceland.

Those 18 months were life-changing. They learned some valuable lessons: that time is precious and they'd rather accumulate life experiences over material goods; to lean into discomfort because growth happens outside their comfort zone; the value of human connection, especially with people from different cultures in varying circumstances; and that following *their heart and doing what they want to do in this life, even if it's different from what everyone else is doing, pays off immensely.*

Once they returned home, it was hard to integrate back into society. The anxiety of having to find new jobs and a source of income quickly set in. They couldn't afford an apartment anymore, so they took on house- and pet-sitting gigs to have a place to live. The job market was incredibly competitive due to many people being affected by layoffs, which made getting interviews extremely difficult. Emma placed immense pressure on herself to find a job and felt pressure from her family as well. When the stress became too much, she'd often break down in tears.

Eventually, Emma landed another good-paying job, and her husband has been building his own company. Their plan is to keep house- and pet-sitting to build their savings back up a bit more before securing their own housing. While the past two years have been a mix of emotions with highs and lows, the highs have far outweighed everything else. Their lives are forever changed; they've grown into better versions of themselves and have these incredible memories to reflect on. When they look back, Emma knows they'll be proud that instead of letting what they "should" be doing at their age dictate the direction of their lives, they did what they wanted to do in this one life they have.

After seeing Emma and her husband's adventures, Ren and Lucas were inspired to travel the world more themselves. They used their paid time off to travel extensively, immersed themselves in other cultures, and observed how people in different countries live. She posted their travels on social media, which caught the attention of Chloe, one of her childhood friends, leading them to reconnect.

Chloe shared how her priorities had shifted over the years, from chasing the American Dream to focusing more on her love of travel. She revealed that several years ago, she had gotten married but began to question whether she was truly happy. For a while, she went through the motions, trying to convince herself that she was content. On paper, she had a great life and marriage, but she realized she wasn't fulfilled and felt sad all the time. She didn't recognize the person she had become and came to the difficult realization that she wasn't living authentically.

Chloe and her husband had gone to the same high school but reconnected years later in the city, quickly hitting it off. They jumped right into dating and began building a life together. Eventually, as their friends started getting married, buying houses, and having kids, marriage felt like the natural next step for them too. They got married, bought a condo together, and began planning for their future.

When they bought the condo, it made sense financially since they planned to live in the city for the foreseeable future. However, her husband struggled to contribute financially, which made paying the mortgage more challenging and worsened their relationship problems. Relying on Chloe's income to cover the mortgage and maintain the home, while trying to keep up with their friends' lifestyles, became increasingly difficult without his financial contributions.

Eventually, their relationship problems became impossible to ignore, and Chloe realized she wasn't married to the right person. Deciding to divorce was difficult—not just because of the stigma, but because her friends and family adored her partner. Still, she knew deep down that staying together would mean sacrificing both of their happiness. She couldn't justify building a future on a foundation that no longer felt right, so she made the painful choice to end their marriage.

At 30 years old, Chloe found herself divorced and selling the condo they had bought together. The year that followed was filled with shame and guilt, both from herself and others. All she could do was pick herself up and move forward into her next chapter.

With time, you grow and evolve. Chloe is now in a new, fulfilling relationship and has stopped chasing what everyone else is doing, instead forging a path that feels right for her. She and her partner rent a condo with no interest in buying a house–a decision that surprises people. But for them, homeownership isn't a top priority right now. They prioritize spending a few months each year visiting family in Europe and traveling the world, a lifestyle made more attainable without the financial burden of a mortgage.

Chloe used to care deeply about what others thought. Two years ago, not owning a home would have made her feel like her life was falling apart simply because she didn't have what her friends had. But the pressure has faded as she's grown more comfortable in her own life. She understands her path looks different from almost everyone she knows, and she's okay with that. While her friends own beautiful homes, many can't afford to travel the way she can. Neither path is better than the other—they've just chosen to prioritize different things.

Now, Chloe loves herself, her partner, and the life they're building together. Her version of the American Dream is simple: a loving, fulfilling relationship, going to bed happy every night, spending time with family and friends, and traveling the world. She just turned 34, and while she may not own much by traditional standards, she feels incredibly lucky to already be *living the life she dreamed of. It took hard choices and a lot of growth to get here, but she couldn't be happier.*

Lessons from Ren's childhood and her friends taught her that life doesn't have to follow a standardized script, and she doesn't have to chase traditional markers of success. Homeownership, impressive careers, and accumulating material possessions aren't the only measures of a meaningful life. Prioritizing deep relationships, seeking new experiences, and cultivating a peaceful, joyful life can be just as fulfilling. The sooner she and her friends quieted the voices telling them what they should be doing and began pursuing their own paths—ones that aligned with their unique values, hopes, and ideals—the sooner they started truly living the dream.

In summary...

• **The American Dream has evolved over time:** Originally popularized during the Great Depression by James Truslow Adams, the concept emphasized equality and the pursuit of a better, richer life for all. Over time, it shifted toward consumerism, material wealth, and individualism, diverging from its original ethos.

• **History has shaped the cornerstone ideals:** Post-war suburban homeownership became central to the American Dream, symbolizing independence and financial success. Advances in consumer goods fueled materialism and societal pressure to acquire "more, new, and better" items. Education emerged as a critical pathway to upward mobility and securing high-paying jobs.

• **Younger generations are redefining the American Dream:** Many are questioning traditional milestones like homeownership, costly college degrees, and corporate ladder climbing. Instead, they prioritize happiness, flexibility, and meaningful experiences, embracing paths that align with their values rather than societal expectations.

Thought Starters

1. What parts of your life align with the traditional American Dream? How does your life differ?

2. In your own version of the American Dream, what do you value most and what are your top priorities? Does your current life align with this dream?

3. What can you change or improve to get closer to your American Dream?

CHAPTER TEN

SMILE LINES

*"Your face is marked with lines of life, put there by love
and laughter, suffering and tears. It's beautiful..."*

-Lynsay Sands

Ren's mom was beautiful inside and out, but she often struggled to see herself in the same light. Her insecurities began in childhood because she was teased about her appearance. Kids would make fun of her "chicken legs" or call her a "witch" because of the bump on the bridge of her nose. As she got older, her concerns deepened. She and her friends frequently discussed the challenges of aging and daydreamed about ways to fix their perceived imperfections. But to Ren, her mother was perfect.

Unfortunately, no matter how lovingly others looked at her mom, she remained her harshest critic, only appreciating the way she looked after the fact. Flipping through old photo albums, she would admire her hair, skin, or figure from back in the day—yet in those very moments, she would have been critical of her appearance. This taught Ren a valuable lesson: we often scrutinize our imperfections, only to later long for the features we once had.

As Ren rebuilt her life and pursued happiness, she noticed herself falling into the same pattern of critiquing her appearance as she aged. She knew she didn't want to repeat that cycle and instead wanted to embrace herself today. Determined to change her perspective, she made a conscious effort to shift her mindset.

When self-criticism crept in, she replaced those thoughts with self-compassion. Rather than fixating on quick fixes, she explored natural ways to age gracefully. Most importantly, she redirected her focus from how she looked to what truly mattered—her wisdom, her character, and how she treated others.

Bit by bit, her efforts made her happier and more optimistic about growing older, and she found herself less concerned about her appearance. However, adopting this mindset hasn't been easy. It's a daily battle—one that requires her to actively challenge negative thoughts and reframe her perspective. While it takes consistent effort, her new outlook has profoundly improved her daily life, bringing more joy to the way she sees herself and how she approaches life.

When we're young, it feels as though our youth will last forever, but eventually, time passes us by and we grow older. While the process of aging can be incredibly beautiful, it's rarely perceived this way. Instead of focusing on all we've experienced in life, we tend to fixate on our physical transformation. Our hair starts to turn gray, the creases in our skin become more pronounced, and our bodies don't move or look quite like they used to. The beauty of the life we've lived becomes a distant memory, and the worry over getting older comes into focus, making us want to turn back time and recapture our youth.

This negative view of aging is deeply ingrained in American society. Older adults are often stereotyped and perceived as incompetent, unattractive, weak, and of lower status, resulting in many being discriminated against as they age. As a result, most of us judge ourselves more harshly and worry about growing older.

Aging is villainized while youth and beauty are glorified, pushing many to stay "young" as long as possible. Constant messages about the value of youth make us want to appear younger. Women aged 25 to 44 are most concerned about aging, but this anxiety is now affecting younger generations. This desire for youthfulness fuels the multibillion-dollar beauty industry, convincing us that makeup, anti-aging products, and cosmetic procedures can help us achieve eternal youth.

The practice of hiding signs of aging dates back to 1500 BC when Egyptians used henna to conceal gray hair. Later, the Greeks and Romans used plant extracts to dye their hair as well. A few hundred years later, companies like L'Oréal and Clairol introduced more permanent dyes, a variety of color options, and the ability to dye hair at home. In the 1940s, only 7 percent of American women dyed their hair, but by the 1970s, that figure had grown to 40 percent. In the 1980s, Clairol began marketing to women's anxieties about aging, calling gray hair dull, drab, and "the ruination of romance." Today, the majority of women dye their hair, and it has become a standard part of many beauty routines.

To minimize our imperfections as we age, some turn to cosmetic procedures and plastic surgery. While most people aren't getting cosmetic work done, the number of those who do has grown, and social media can make it seem like "everyone is doing it." We are bombarded online with edited and filtered images portraying idealized versions of beauty and have more visibility into the lives of people who get elective procedures, which can leave us feeling inadequate in comparison. A recent study showed how powerful social media can be; the more time you spend on social media, the more likely you are to want to alter your appearance.

As we age, everyone should be able to do what they want to their bodies freely and without judgment. As long as these choices help us feel comfortable in our own skin, rather than conforming to arbitrary beauty ideals, they can significantly improve our well-being and confidence. Increased confidence can have a positive ripple effect on our relationships, careers, and overall happiness.

But what if you don't want to keep up with society's beauty standards as you age? What if you decide to embrace natural aging, instead? In a world that expects perpetual youth, it can be challenging to reject societal expectations and embrace the aging process.

Being anti-aging

is a rule of behavior

that individuals prefer to conform to on the condition that they believe...

most people in their network try to avoid aging

most people in their network think they ought to avoid aging too

Adopting a positive attitude toward aging can counter society's negative perceptions. Instead of scrutinizing ourselves and feeling the need to make adjustments, shifting our mindset about aging can help us be happier and live longer. Some of the biggest concerns people have about aging are wrinkles and gray hair. Reframing these as positive can help us cope. For instance, wrinkles are amplified by expressiveness; smiling, laughing, crying, and frowning all contribute. If we think about emotions as an important part of life and what makes us human, we can view these lines as the byproducts of our humanity and a life well-lived.

On a societal level, changing the portrayal of older adults in the media is crucial. The media often reinforces stereotypes about aging, which is why organizations such as Hollywood, Health & Society (HHS) are working to ensure realistic depictions of aging in shows and movies. Seeing older people's stories, told with empathy and substance, can help lessen anxiety around aging and dismantle stereotypes.

Encouraging intergenerational relationships can also foster a more positive view of aging. When young people interact with older adults, they gain a realistic understanding of growing older, reducing anxiety. Spending time with older family members, neighbors, or in spaces they frequent can build empathy and shift perceptions. Policies that promote intergenerational connections, like combining nurseries, youth clubs, and nursing homes, benefit both generations—providing young people with a realistic view and offering older adults companionship during a time that can be lonely.

Until this becomes the norm, those who choose to celebrate aging and reject the anti-aging narrative must navigate social pressure and the temptation to fit in by striving to look younger. While we can begin practicing a more positive outlook on aging in our daily lives, society's expectations still have a long way to go before we start to genuinely accept and appreciate getting older.

As time passed, Ren became increasingly fascinated by society's perception of aging, particularly when it came to gray hair. As she and her friends' hair began to turn, it became more noticeable when someone chose to embrace their natural color. Ren had always felt the need to dye her hair, but she admired those who didn't. One person she had always looked up to was Brooke, her college roommate, who exuded confidence and had fully embraced her silver hair over the years.

For years, Ren hesitated to mention Brooke's hair, fearing she might offend her by drawing attention to it. But eventually, curiosity got the best of her, and she worked up the courage to ask. To her surprise, Brooke was happy she noticed and eager to talk about it. Now in her mid-30s, most of Brooke's hair had turned silver. She often realized she was the only one her age with naturally gray hair, since most people chose to dye it.

Some of Brooke's earliest memories revolved around hair dye. As a child, she watched her mom and a friend regularly dye each other's hair in the bathroom sink. Every week, her grandmother visited, and her mom helped her perm and color her hair as well. Brooke found it interesting to see them trying to hold back time by covering their grays—something she now prefers not to do herself.

Her hair has evolved over the years, and now she loves how the different shades blend together, but she didn't always feel that way. At 18 years old, she spotted her first gray strand. Sitting in her car, she caught a glimpse of a wiry silver hair in the rearview mirror. Panicked, she immediately pulled it out, convinced it was too soon for her hair to be turning.

By 30 years old, her hair was visibly gray, yet she never felt compelled to dye it. She's not entirely sure why—perhaps it was because she had come to terms with the fact she would probably go gray early, since it runs in her family. Knowing it was inevitable, she decided to embrace it. The time and money required to dye her hair also deterred her. She had other things she'd rather invest in.

She's noticed that people rarely comment on her hair, likely out of fear she'd take offense. Society has conditioned us to view gray hair as undesirable, to the point where even mentioning it feels taboo. Still, she wishes that if people liked her hair, they would say so. Once, a stranger at a grocery store complimented her hair color, and it made her day.

While Brooke loves her natural hair, she hopes to maintain her confidence as she ages. She's not interested in altering her appearance, choosing instead to embrace herself as she is. In a world where many women feel pressured to cover their grays and dye their hair, she hopes to be a small source of inspiration for anyone considering embracing their natural hair, showing them that they can do it too.

Over the years, Ren spoke to her friends about aging—like in her conversation with Brooke—but became increasingly curious about how others, especially those a bit older than her, viewed the process. She rarely interacted with people outside her age group—except for Iris, her former professor. Even after graduating, she and Iris stayed in touch, their conversations flowing effortlessly from one topic to the next. Eventually, their discussions turned to aging.

Iris, now 49 years old, admitted that she couldn't even look at pictures of herself without focusing on her flaws. She used to admire her bright smile and blue eyes, but now all she saw were her heavy eyelids and areas she felt needed cosmetic work. This surprised Ren, as Iris was one of the most inspiring and confident people she knew—someone who could lift you up in a single conversation and make you feel like you could change the world. If anything, Ren had always aspired to be more like her.

Iris didn't see herself the same way Ren did, though. As she got older, she was concerned that the world perceived her differently. Though she knew her spouse loved her unconditionally, she still worried if he would find her attractive as she aged. She also sensed that society saw her in a new light, which saddened her. She often asked herself, Why can't I embrace getting older? The aging process had been challenging, and staying positive about it took effort.

It began to bother her to the point where she started considering Botox, fillers, or even a facelift. She had once opposed these procedures, mainly because she had never been exposed to them. But as discussions about such treatments became more common among her friends—some of whom had already tried them—she found herself reconsidering options she had once dismissed. What was once unthinkable now seemed like a possibility.

For now, Iris has no immediate plans for drastic changes but isn't ruling them out. If she decides to move forward, she wants to be confident in her decision and make it for herself, not because of societal pressure. The main reason she hasn't made a change yet is her commitment to resisting negative thoughts about aging. The people in her life help lift her up, making it easier to love herself as she is. She's focused on shifting her mindset, prioritizing health over vanity, and viewing aging as a privilege, not a burden. Still, it's a daily struggle—a constant pep talk she hopes will improve over time, so she can embrace herself more fully as she ages, no matter how she looks.

Ren noticed how much societal expectations had impacted her mom, Iris, and even herself, which frustrated her. The more stories she heard from her loved one's about their struggles with their looks, the more annoyed she became with how society was eroding everyone's self-image. She often ranted about beauty standards and the media to her friends. During one of her tirades, her friend Mila chimed in, sharing these pressures had affected her and her mom as well.

Mila thinks the world of her mom, but she noticed a stark contrast in how her mom viewed herself. When Mila showed her an adorable photo of them laughing together at a wedding, all her mom could focus on was how "horrible" she thought she looked. While Mila saw a beautiful moment between them, her mom fixated on perceived imperfections. It saddened Mila that society had made her mom feel anything but beautiful because, to Mila, she was idyllic.

Over the years, Mila's mom would make unkind comments about herself. The wrinkles on her face were unacceptable. Her arms were too jiggly when she'd wave. She wouldn't smile too big in pictures because the skin under her eyes would crease, and her teeth were too crooked, so she'd soften her smile into a lifeless grin.

But what her mom doesn't realize is that when she's gone, Mila will wish she could see her smile one last time—a big, toothy grin that makes her eyes crease ten times over. She'll wish she could squeeze her mom's arm or watch her wave hello just once more. When her mom is gone, Mila will stare for hours at that picture her mom doesn't like—the one where they're caught in a fit of laughter—and wish they could laugh together one more time. When Mila thinks of her mom, she'll remember how she made the world brighter and better just by being in it.

While Mila wishes her mom could see herself through her eyes, she doesn't blame her for not liking the way she looks—not for a second. Mila falls into the trap of thinking she's not beautiful too. It's hard to see her own beauty, especially when her judgment is clouded by society's standards of what is beautiful. It's difficult to recognize her own worth when she's constantly bombarded on social media with images of celebrities and influencers who never seem to age. Society teaches us that aging is something to fear, and people are told they need Botox, fillers, and facelifts to stay beautiful.

It feels like everyone Mila knows has Botox now, and it has become the norm. The more people in her life that have it, the more tempting it becomes for Mila, and the more she considers it herself. But if she's honest, she doesn't actually want it. She fully supports others doing what feels right for them and celebrates with her friends when they choose those options, but she has no interest in it for herself. Mila doesn't want to limit her expressiveness or have her beauty defined by whether a procedure has worn off or not. She never wants to look in the mirror and feel like her natural self is less than, and she doesn't want that for the women in her life either.

When it comes to aging, Mila is focused on what works best for her. She prefers to invest in taking care of her skin rather than injecting anything into her face. Instead of trying to fix her wrinkles, she wants to embrace them as a natural part of aging. She wants to genuinely believe that her laugh lines and crow's feet exist because she has laughed hard and often, which is beautiful. So for now, she is making a daily effort to see aging as a gift. She knows it won't always be easy to embrace her appearance or body as she gets older, and she may feel tempted to "fix" her imperfections, but she also knows she owes it to herself to love the person she is becoming.

Having these conversations helped Ren realize that aging is a universal experience, and most of us are bombarded by social pressures that easily infiltrate our minds, causing pervasive thoughts. She came to understand that self-love is an ongoing, daily practice that requires dedication, and that the choice of what we do with our bodies is ultimately ours to make. Regardless of what each person decides is right for them, one thing she feels adamant about is the importance of being kind to ourselves and giving ourselves grace as we grow older. The world already has incredibly high standards and is overly critical of us as we age, which is challenging enough—we shouldn't make it harder on ourselves. At the end of the day, we need to find the beauty in the inevitability of getting older, build ourselves up, and celebrate as we age. Because, odds are, those imperfections are a figment of our imagination, distorted by societal expectations, when in reality, and through our loved ones' eyes, we are everything and more.

In summary...

- **Aging is often viewed negatively in society:** There is a pervasive negative perception of aging, leading to discrimination and stereotypes against older adults. As time passes, people tend to focus on physical changes, such as gray hair and wrinkles, rather than appreciating the beauty of a life well-lived.
- **Youth and beauty are glorified:** Society places a high value on youth and beauty, prompting many to conceal signs of aging and pursue a youthful appearance through products, cosmetic procedures, and other anti-aging measures.
- **We must shift perceptions around getting older:** Rejecting societal beauty standards and embracing ourselves as we age can enhance happiness and well-being. More accurate media portrayals and fostering intergenerational relationships can help reframe aging as a positive experience, reducing anxiety and breaking down stereotypes.

Thought Starters

1. How do you feel about aging? What aspects of getting older do you embrace and what worries you?

2. When it comes to aging and getting older, what outlook would you like to have? How does your current mindset align with this ideal or not?

3. What are some steps you can take to infuse how you'd ideally like to think about aging into your everyday life?

Part III
UPWARD

CHAPTER ELEVEN

BEYOND THE IMAGINABLE

"We should all open our eyes and minds to the limitless possibilities the world has to offer."
-Lisa Messenger

Ren stood on her back patio, a warm mug of hot cocoa cradled in her hands, gazing out at the California coastline as the sun set. The sky was painted in soft shades of pink and orange, and the salty breeze brushed across her face. She was living her dream life. Whether reading a book in her sunny backyard, spending time with Lucas, or laughing with her close friends who deeply understood her, Ren often found herself moved to tears by the overwhelming gratitude she felt. *I'm so, so lucky,* she often thought to herself.

But this life wasn't just a stroke of luck. It had been a decade in the making—a journey filled with deep reflection, relentless self-work, intentional choices, ferocious courage, and unwavering effort. Ren had taken small steps toward her vision every day. The progress was so gradual that it might have gone unnoticed by anyone not paying close attention, but she stayed focused, forging ahead until she arrived at her dream—the life she had envisioned for herself back in grad school ten years earlier.

Ren and her friends—who had been on their own respective journeys to reclaim their lives—often found themselves reflecting on their newfound peace and happiness together. When much of *life is spent following the crowd, succumbing to pressure, or fulfilling others' expectations, it can be difficult to imagine what life might look like if you start living for yourself. The weight of obligations that don't bring joy or the presence of people who drain your energy begins to feel like a reality you're forced to accept. But when you finally start making decisions based on what truly makes you happy, the resulting peace and joy can be quite moving.*

Prioritizing your own interests significantly impacts day-to-day happiness. People are happiest when their time is spent doing things they want to do rather than things they feel obligated to do. Happiness in any given moment often depends on whether a person is acting out of free will or pressure. When someone chooses to live according to their own values, hopes, and dreams—without being swayed by the expectations of others—their life feels richer, more meaningful, and deeply fulfilling. This is exactly what Ren did.

The most profound change in Ren was her newfound love and appreciation for herself. For so long, she had carried the belief that she was unlikeable—a lesson ingrained in her throughout childhood. This belief caused her to chase love and acceptance by prioritizing others' wants and needs over her own. But eventually, she came to the conclusion that if life meant constantly appeasing everyone around her at the expense of her own happiness, she didn't have a lifetime left in her to give.

As she learned to stand on her own, Ren discovered something she had never known before: it didn't matter if anyone else liked her, as long as she liked herself. Instead of giving love freely to others, as she had been—only to be overlooked or taken for granted—she began to keep that love for herself. In those moments when she stood firmly on her own, she no longer craved or needed validation from others because she had finally found it within herself.

Ren's journey was profoundly shaped by the love and lessons passed down from her mom. Losing her was a deeply painful experience, but her sacrifices became important life lessons and the driving force behind everything Ren achieved.

When reflecting on her mother's final moments, Ren cherished a conversation that stayed with her forever—a conversation she had never shared with anyone until now. In those last hours, after weeks of wrestling with deep regret, her mom turned to her and smiled softly for the first time in weeks. "I've realized something," she said. "Raising you and your siblings was the greatest joy of my life. I might not have gone to Italy or seen the northern lights, but I didn't waste my time... my time was very well spent because of you." She paused, her voice growing more stern. "But please, Ren... promise me you'll remember to do what you want in life."

Ren nodded with tears welling up in her eyes, "You don't have to worry anymore, Mom. I will."

In her final moments, Sofia was no longer burdened by regret. While she could have lived more fully on her own terms, her life held meaning far beyond her unrealized dreams. She had passed on lessons that would guide her children to pursue their own happiness and live the lives they had always dreamed of.

A few hours after that heartfelt conversation, Sofia passed away, and Ren felt a bittersweet sense of relief, knowing her mom had finally found peace.

Now, as Ren sat on her back patio, reflecting on all the work she had done and the life she had created since those final moments, she desperately wished she could show her mom the beautiful life she had built. Since that was no longer possible, Ren gazed up at the stars with tears in her eyes, hoping her mom was looking down on her, smiling—knowing that every dream Ren pursued and every moment of joy she cultivated was because of her.

At last, you've learned everything Ren knows about how to stand alone in a world of powerful social influence. Now, all that's left is to channel your inner Ren—and go chase your dreams, too. Sofia would be proud that you did.

ACKNOWLEDGMENTS

Thank you to my own mom who has been a guiding light in my life. Her unwavering support, love, and wisdom have been the foundation of everything I've achieved.

To John, my partner in life and a tremendous source of happiness: together, we've built a life that surpasses every dream I ever had for myself.

To the women who shared their stories with me: there are too many to name individually, but you know who you are. Your vulnerability and bravery are the soul of this book. Thank you for trusting me, for enriching these pages, and for cheering me on throughout this process.

To Dr. Sara Truebridge: thank you for believing this story was worth telling and for insisting we share it with the world. Your faith in me and this project has meant everything.

To Scottie and Meg McAdams, the bridge to Sara and my dear friends who wholeheartedly support my farfetched dreams: thank you for your gift of connecting hearts and minds. Your small acts of kindness played a pivotal role in this journey.

To Dr. Matt Moehle and Dr. Amy Gray at EDLINKS® Press: your thoughtful reviews and honest feedback were invaluable. Your insights helped shape this book into what it is today.

To Bekah Martin and Bryn Smith: my trusted advisors, thank you for being the first people to read the book. Your support and perspective were invaluable in shaping the final version of this story.

To Savannah Benavides, my editor: Your talent and dedication transformed my writing into something far more beautiful and coherent than I could have achieved on my own. Your editing elevated this story to new heights.

And to Annie Frisoli: Thank you for introducing me to Savannah and for believing in me from the moment we met more than ten years ago—and every day since.

NOTES

INTRODUCTION

Page 3: **One of the biggest regrets people have at the end of their lives:** Ware, B. (2019). Top five regrets of the dying: a life transformed by the dearly departing. Alexandria (New South Wales): Hay House.

Page 3: **haunted by regrets:** Davidai, S., & Gilovich, T. (2018). The ideal road not taken: The self-discrepancies involved in people's most enduring regrets. Emotion, 18(3), 439.

Page 4: **powerful and invisible forces that influence us:** Berger, J. (2016). Invisible influence: The hidden forces that shape behavior. Simon and Schuster.

Page 5: **idea of standing alone from Brené Brown:** Brown, B. (2017). Braving the Wilderness: The Quest for True Belonging and the Courage to Stand Alone. Random House.

CHAPTER ONE: POWERFUL & INVISIBLE INFLUENCES

page 9 **"Never mistake the power of influence.":** Rohn, J. (n.d.). Resolutions. Retrieved from leaderinfluence.net.

Page 9 **powerful influences:** Berger, J. (2016). Invisible influence: The hidden forces that shape behavior. Simon and Schuster.

Page 9 **natural desire to belong:** Baumeister, R. F., & Leary, M. R. (2017). The need to belong: Desire for interpersonal attachments as a fundamental human motivation. Interpersonal development, 57-89.

Page 9 **we inherited this biological yearning from our ancestors:** Moffett, M. W. (2013). Human identity and the evolution of societies. Human Nature, 24, 219-267.

Page 10 **but it can still be deeply painful:** MacDonald, G., & Leary, M. R. (2005). Why does social exclusion hurt? The relationship between social and physical pain. Psychological Bulletin, 131(2), 202–223.

Page 10 **our parents begin to impose rules, values, beliefs, traditions, and expectations onto us:** Tsabary, S. (2023). The Parenting Map: Step-by-Step Solutions to Consciously Create the Ultimate Parent-Child Relationship. HarperCollins.

Page 10 **use a mental shortcut called social proof:** Cialdini, R. B., Wosinska, W., Barrett, D. W., Butner, J., & Gornik-Durose, M. (1999). Compliance with a request in two cultures: The differential influence of social proof and commitment/consistency on collectivists and individualists. Personality and Social Psychology Bulletin, 25(10), 1242-1253.

Page 10 **observing what everyone else is doing, and act accordingly by imitating the people around us:** Over, H., & Carpenter, M. (2013). The social side of imitation. Child Development Perspectives, 7(1), 6–11.

Page 10 **become social chameleons:** van Schaik, J. E., & Hunnius, S. (2016). Little chameleons: The development of social mimicry during early childhood. Journal of Experimental Child Psychology, 147, 71–81.

Page 10 **Famous studies have shown:** Asch, S. E. (1956). Studies of independence and conformity: A minority of one against a unanimous majority. Psychological Monographs: General and Applied, 70(9), 1–70.

Page 13 **research by Dr. Cristina Bicchieri:** Bicchieri, C. (2016). Norms in the wild: How to diagnose, measure, and change social norms. Oxford University Press.

Page 13 **"A social norm is a rule of behavior that individuals prefer to conform to on the condition that they believe...":** Bicchieri, C. (2006). The grammar of society: The nature and dynamics of social norms. Cambridge University Press.

Page 14 **When we follow a social norm, we are often greeted with positive reactions and approval:** Cialdini, R. B., & Goldstein, N. J. (2004). Social influence: Compliance and conformity. Annual Review of Psychology, 55(1), 591-621..

Page 14 **These positive interactions release dopamine:** Krach, S., Paulus, F. M., Bodden, M., & Kircher, T. (2010). The rewarding nature of social interactions. Frontiers in Behavioral Neuroscience, 4, 1141.

Page 14 **Our brains love predictability:** Worthen, J. B., Coats, S., McGlynn, R. P., & Rossano, M. J. (2007). Cognitive factors in the prediction of liking of social groups: Prototypes, predictability and familiarity. New research on social perception, 161-179.

Page 14 **35,000 decisions every single day:** Zhang, X., & Zhu, Q. (2021). Difficult choices: Exploring basic reasons of difficult choices. Journal of Frontiers of Society, Science and Technology, 3(5), 182–191.

Page 14 **other people will react negatively to us if we go against the grain:** Van Kleef, G. A., Wanders, F., Stamkou, E., & Homan, A. C. (2015). The social dynamics of breaking the rules: Antecedents and consequences of norm-violating behavior. Current Opinion in Psychology, 6, 25–31.

Page 14 **worries can be real or perceived:** Bicchieri, C. (2016). Norms in the wild: How to diagnose, measure, and change social norms. Oxford University Press.

Page 15 **our brains emit a neurological error signal:** Kim, B.-R., Liss, A., Rao, M., Singer, Z., & Compton, R. J. (2011). Social deviance activates the brain's error-monitoring system. Cognitive, Affective, & Behavioral Neuroscience, 12(1), 65–73.

Page 15 **People pleasers tend to have painful childhood experiences:** Walker, P. (2018). Complex PTSD: From surviving to thriving. Tantor Audio.

Page 15 **causes a surge in dopamine:** Krach, S. (2010). The rewarding nature of social interactions. Frontiers in Behavioral Neuroscience, 4(22).

Page 15 **it's easy to convince ourselves that we've been thoughtful and deliberate:** Fraseur, S. J. (2020). The irrational mind: How to fight back against the hidden forces that affect decision making. Spencer Fraseur.

Page 15 **we are on autopilot most of the time:** Killingsworth, M. A., & Gilbert, D. T. (2010). A wandering mind is an unhappy mind. Science, 330(6006), 932–932.

Page 15 **following the norm when it doesn't align with our values:** Rogers, C. R. (1961). On becoming a person. Houghton Mifflin.

Page 16 **release of dopamine:** Krach, S. (2010). The rewarding nature of social interactions. Frontiers in Behavioral Neuroscience, 4(22).

Page 16 **We mold ourselves into someone we're not:** Beck, M. N. (2021). The way of integrity: Finding the path to your true self. Penguin Life.

Page 16 **belonging in this world:** Baumeister, R. F., & Leary, M. R. (2017). The need to belong: Desire for interpersonal attachments as a fundamental human motivation. Interpersonal development, 57-89.

CHAPTER TWO: STAND ALONE

page 21 **"It takes nothing to join the crowd. It takes everything to stand alone.":** Hansen, H. F. (n.d.).. It takes nothing to join the crowd. It takes everything to stand alone. Retrieved from goodreads.com.

page 22 **take ourselves off autopilot and turn inward:** Paulson, S., Davidson, R., Jha, A., & Kabat-Zinn, J. (2013). Becoming conscious: The science of mindfulness. Annals of the New York Academy of Sciences, 1303(1), 87–104.

page 22 **we can get closer to becoming our true and ideal selves:** Rogers, C. R. (1959). A theory of therapy, personality and interpersonal relationships as developed in the client-centered framework. In S. Koch (Ed.), Psychology: A study of a science. Vol. 3: Formulations of the person and the social context (pp. 184–256). McGraw-Hill.

page 22 **our beliefs aren't clear or accessible to us on the surface:** Alcock, J. E. (2022). Belief and the cognitive unconscious. The Cognitive Unconscious: The First Half Century, 306.

page 22 **Our unconscious beliefs have a profound impact on our behavior:** Freud, S. (1915). The unconscious. In S. Freud (Ed.), General psychological theory: Papers on metapsychology (pp. 116–150). Macmillan Publishing Company.

page 22 **become more aware by consciously evaluating our beliefs:** Bicchieri, C. (2017). Norms in the wild: How to diagnose, measure, and change social norms. Oxford University Press.

page 23 **evaluate our lives through a new lens to make decisions:** Karelaia, N., & Reb, J. (2015). Improving decision making through mindfulness. In Mindfulness in organizations: Foundations, research, and applications (pp. 163). Springer.

page 23 **imagine we're sitting on a balcony observing ourselves:** Van Gordon, W., Shonin, E., Gilbert, P., Garcia-Campayo, J., & Gallardo, L. (2023). Mindfulness of happiness. Mindfulness, 14(3), 757–760.

page 23 **we have the opportunity to alter the trajectory of our lives with every choice we make:** Weiss, J. W., Weiss, D. J., & Edwards, W. (2009). Big decisions, little decisions: The hierarchy of everyday life. In A science of decision making: The legacy of Ward Edwards (pp. 451–459). Cambridge University Press.

page 23 **Being mindful helps us notice:** Siegel, R. D., Germer, C. K., & Olendzki, A. (2009). Mindfulness: What is it? Where did it come from? In Clinical handbook of mindfulness (pp. 17–35). Springer.

page 23 **Dr. Bicchieri refers to these individuals as "first movers":** Bicchieri, C. (2017). Norms in the wild: How to diagnose, measure, and change social norms. Oxford University Press.

page 24-26 **each condition outlined by Dr. Bicchieri**: Bicchieri, C. (2017). Norms in the wild: How to diagnose, measure, and change social norms. Oxford University Press.

CHAPTER THREE: CONVEY, SWAY, AND STAY

page 31 **"If you would persuade, you must appeal to interest rather than intellect"**: Franklin, B. (n.d.). Quotation Details. Retrieved from quotationspage.com

page 33 **opening yourself up to varied opinions, judgments, or criticisms**: Van Kleef, G. A., Wanders, F., Stamkou, E., & Homan, A. C. (2015). The social dynamics of breaking the rules: Antecedents and consequences of norm-violating behavior. Current Opinion in Psychology, 6, 25-31.

page 33 **Our lives are an elaborate, interconnected network**: Settersten, R. A. (2018). Relationships in time and the life course: The significance of linked lives. In The Study of Human Development (pp. 61-67). Routledge.

page 33 **can cause negative reactions ranging from judgment, criticism, gossip, and scolding to withholding love**: Van Kleef, G. A., Wanders, F., Stamkou, E., & Homan, A. C. (2015). The social dynamics of breaking the rules: Antecedents and consequences of norm-violating behavior. Current Opinion in Psychology, 6, 25-31.

page 33 **challenges their beliefs and expectations**: Van Kleef, G. A., Wanders, F., Stamkou, E., & Homan, A. C. (2015). The social dynamics of breaking the rules: Antecedents and consequences of norm-violating behavior. Current Opinion in Psychology, 6, 25-31.

page 34 **direct and honest communication is key**: Jansen, F., & Janssen, D. (2013). Effects of directness in bad-news e-mails and voicemails. The Journal of Business Communication (1973), 50(4), 362-382.

page 34 **convoluting the message**: Heath, C., & Heath, D. (2007). Made to stick: Why some ideas survive and others die. Random House.

page 35 **Persuading people that a decision is right for you begins with trust**: Cialdini, R. (2016). Pre-suasion: A revolutionary way to influence and persuade. Simon and Schuster.

page 35 **Knowing what those close to us value most can help us communicate our plan to go against the norm**: Grant, A., Sanders, F., & Denaker, S. (2016). Originals: how non-conformists move the world. Unabridged. New York, Penguin Audio.

page 35 **first share our plans to go against the norm with the people we trust the most:** Grant, A., Sanders, F., & Denaker, S. (2016). Originals: how non-conformists move the world. Unabridged. New York, Penguin Audio.

page 36 **boost their confidence in you by letting them know of other people's support:** Cialdini, R. (2016). Pre-suasion: A revolutionary way to influence and persuade. Simon and Schuster.

page 36 **language focused on "we" and "us":** Cialdini, Robert B. (2021). Influence, New and Expanded: The Psychology of Persuasion. New York: HarperCollins.

page 36 **You can do your part to make repairs:** Gottman, J. M. (2011). The science of trust: Emotional attunement for couples. WW Norton & Company.

page 37 **Decisions that align with our values, beliefs, and goals feel better:** Karelaia, N., & Reb, J. (2015). Improving decision making through mindfulness. Mindfulness in organizations: Foundations, research, and applications, 163.

CHAPTER FOUR: HEART OF THE MATTER

page 41 **"Sometimes we create our own heartbreak with expectations":** Lovely Quotes. Retrieved from Pinterest.com

page 42 **we mindlessly and silently place these expectations onto our partners, children, friends, family, and colleagues:** Anderson, L. D., Banks, S. R., & Owens, M. L. (2019). Silent agreements: How to free your relationships of unspoken expectations. Random House.

page 42 **We assume most people will think and behave similarly to us:** Ross, L., Greene, D., & House, P. (1977). The false consensus effect: An egocentric bias in social perception and attribution processes. Journal of Experimental Social Psychology, 13, 279–301.

page 43 **we tend to have emotional reactions:** Van Kleef, G. A., Wanders, F., Stamkou, E., & Homan, A. C. (2015). The social dynamics of breaking the rules: Antecedents and consequences of norm-violating behavior. Current Opinion in Psychology, 6, 25-31.

page 43 **Several researchers propose three ways to cope with unfulfilled expectations:** Pietzsch, M. C., & Pinquart, M. (2023). Predicting coping with expectation violations: combining the ViolEx Model and the Covariation Principle. Frontiers in Psychology, 14, 1152261.

page 45 **especially since saying no is difficult for many:** Givi, J., & Kirk, C. P. (2024). Saying no: The negative ramifications from invitation declines are less severe than we think. Journal of Personality and Social Psychology, 126(6), 1103.

PROLOGUE: FIRST MOVERS

page 51 **"[First movers] will never influence their peers if news of their deviance does not spread.":** Bicchieri, C. (2016). Norms in the wild: How to diagnose, measure, and change social norms. Oxford University Press.

page 51 **they sometimes keep their stories and experiences to themselves:** Goffman, E. (1959). The presentation of self in everyday life. Bantam Doubleday Dell Publishing Group.

CHAPTER FIVE: GOING THE DISTANCE

page 53 **"Leave home with a big, bright dream. Nurture it into a bigger, brighter reality":** (n.d.). The Key Piece. Retrieved from https://www.ljblegal.com/library/august-2023-key-piece-WEB.pdf

page 55 **Deciding where to live is usually one of the more impactful decisions of your life:** Newport, C. (2016). Deep work: Rules for focused success in a distracted world. Grand Central Publishing.

page 55 **Where we live has a powerful impact on our overall health and happiness:** Brereton, F., Clinch, J. P., & Ferreira, S. (2008). Happiness, geography and the environment. Ecological economics, 65(2), 386-396.

page 55 **coming from a place of privilege:** Bureau, U. C. (2022, July 25). New Data Tool and Research Show Where People Move as Young Adults. Census.gov. Retrieved from https://www.census.gov/library/stories/2022/07/theres-no-place-like-home.html

page 55 **interconnected nature of life, family, work, and relationships:** Settersten, R. A. (2018). Relationships in time and the life course: The significance of linked lives. In The Study of Human Development (pp. 61-67). Routledge.

page 56 **In America, about 6 in 10 young adults live within a 10-mile radius of their hometown, with 8 in 10 living within 100 miles of where they grew up:** Bureau, U. C. (2022, July 25). New Data Tool and Research Show Where People Move as Young Adults. Retrieved from Census.gov, https://www.census.gov/library/stories/2022/07/theres-no-place-like-home.html

page 56 **positive social interactions and having a tight-knit community can be crucial for our well-being and longevity:** Schneider, F. W., Gruman, J. A., & Coutts, L. M. (Eds.). (2012). Applied social psychology: Understanding and addressing social and practical problems. Thousand Oaks, CA: Sage Publications.

page 57 **We tend to form connections and relationships with those who we are physically close to:** Vinney. (2022). What is the proximity principle in psychology. Retrieved from https://www.verywellmind.com/what-is-the-proximity-principle-in-psychology-5195099

page 57 **our hopes and dreams start to revolve around what's possible within that context:** Evans, C. (2016). Moving away or staying local: The role of locality in young people's 'spatial horizons' and career aspirations. Journal of Youth Studies, 19(4), 501-516.

page 57 **we fall into predictable routines:** Ersche, K. D., Lim, T. V., Ward, L. H., Robbins, T. W., & Stochl, J. (2017). Creature of habit: A self-report measure of habitual routines and automatic tendencies in everyday life. Personality and Individual Differences, 116, 73-85.

page 57 **we take our usual route to work and go to the same grocery stores, restaurants, and local shops:** Easter, M. (2023). Scarcity brain: Fix your craving mindset and rewire your habits to thrive with enough. Rodale Books.

page 58 **Our ancestors used to search for answers by exploring unknown lands:** Easter, M. (2023). Scarcity brain: Fix your craving mindset and rewire your habits to thrive with enough. Rodale Books.

page 58 **cause time to pass us by in the blink of an eye:** Hammond, C. (2012). Time warped: Unlocking the mysteries of time perception. House of Anansi.

page 58 **Living close to home is a rule of behavior that individuals prefer to conform to on the condition that…:** Adapted from Bicchieri, C. (2006). The grammar of society: The nature and dynamics of social norms. Cambridge University Press.

page 58 **When we live somewhere for a significant amount of time:** Zajonc, R. B. (1968). Attitudinal effects of mere exposure. Journal of Personality and Social Psychology, 9(2, Pt.2), 1-27.

page 59 **we develop an emotional attachment to that place:** Easthope, H. (2004). A place called home. Housing, theory and society, 21(3), 128-138.

page 59 **we tend to unconsciously give preference to people and places we're familiar with:** Korpela, K. (2012). Place attachment. In S. Clayton (Ed.) The Oxford Handbook of Environmental and Conservation Psychology, 148-163. New York: Oxford University Press.

page 59 **stay close to home:** Clark, W. A., Duque-Calvache, R., & Palomares-Linares, I. (2017). Place attachment and the decision to stay in the neighbourhood. Population, space and place, 23(2), e2001.

page 59 **skeptical of stepping outside of our comfort zone:** Russo-Netzer, P., & Cohen, G. L. (2023). 'If you're uncomfortable, go outside your comfort zone': A novel behavioral 'stretch' intervention supports the well-being of unhappy people. The Journal of Positive Psychology, 18(3), 394-410.

page 59 **A predictable routine keeps us relatively even-keeled:** Nadler, R. S. (1995). Edgework: Stretching boundaries and generalizing experiences. Journal of Experiential Education, 18(1), 52-55.

page 59 **prevent us from pursuing other opportunities that will allow us to grow and transform:** Brown, M. (2008). Comfort zone: Model or metaphor?. Australian Journal of Outdoor Education, 12(1), 3-12.

page 59 **Relocations can be a very stressful life event:** Sandoval, J. (2013). The stress of moving. In Crisis Counseling, Intervention and Prevention in the Schools (pp. 198-211). Routledge.

page 59 **Venturing outside of our hometown broadens our horizon and opens our eyes to what's possible in this world:** Allen, K., & Hollingworth, S. (2013). 'Sticky subjects' or 'cosmopolitan creatives'? Social class, place and urban young people's aspirations for work in the knowledge economy. Urban Studies, 50(3), 499-517.

page 59 **our hopes and dreams start to evolve and expand beyond what we thought was possible for ourselves:** Evans, C. (2016). Moving away or staying local: The role of locality in young people's 'spatial horizons' and career aspirations. Journal of Youth Studies, 19(4), 501-516.

page 60 **slows time down since we can't operate on autopilot:** Hammond, C. (2012). Time warped: Unlocking the mysteries of time perception. House of Anansi.

page 60 **we can feel freer to change our habits and adapt who we are:** Fogg, B. J. (2019). Tiny habits: The small changes that change everything. Eamon Dolan Books.

CHAPTER SIX: NO CONTACT

page 71 **"The bond that links your true family is not one of blood, but of respect and joy in each other's life":** Bach, R. (1984). Illusions: The Adventures of a Reluctant Messiah. Bantam Doubleday Dell Publishing Group.

page 72 **it's the first group we interact with and learn from:** Parke, R. D., & Buriel, R. (2008). Socialization in the family: Ethnic and ecological perspectives. Child and adolescent development: An advanced course, 95-138.

page 72 **these relationships shape who we become:** Benson, J. E., & Johnson, M. K. (2009). Adolescent family context and adult identity formation. Journal of Family Issues, 30(9), 1265-1286.

page 72 **impacts our development and happiness as we age:** Ramos, M. C., Cheng, C.-H. E., Preston, K. S. J., Gottfried, A. W., Guerin, D. W., Gottfried, A. E., Riggio, R. E., & Oliver, P. H. (2022). Positive family relationships across 30 years: Predicting adult health and happiness. Journal of Family Psychology, 36(7), 1216.

page 72-73 **Healthy relationships tend to have more positive interactions than negative ones:** Gottman, J. M. (1994). What predicts divorce? Hillsdale, NJ: Erlbaum.

page 73 **make children feel safe and loved:** Calder, R., & Dakin, P. (2023). Valued, loved and safe: the foundations for healthy individuals and a healthier society. Medical Journal of Australia, 219, S11-S14.

page 73 **Interacting productively with family teaches children how to regulate their emotions and act appropriately in social situations:** Morris, A. S., Silk, J. S., Steinberg, L., Myers, S. S., & Robinson, L. R. (2007). The role of the family context in the development of emotion regulation. Social development, 16(2), 361-388.

page 73 **"blood is thicker than water":** Neyer, F. J., & Lang, F. R. (2003). Blood is thicker than water: kinship orientation across adulthood. Journal of personality and social psychology, 84(2), 310.

page 73 **more than half of Americans have developed expectations that family should come first and be prioritized over all other relationships:** Orth, T. (2022). All on the family: ties, proximity, and estrangement. Retrieved from https://today.yougov.com/society/articles/44817-poll-family-ties-proximity-and-estrangement

page 73 **We are rarely perfectly in-tune:** Gottman, J. M. (2011). The science of trust: Emotional attunement for couples. WW Norton & Company.

page 73 **moments of misalignment with our family members can cause friction and lead to hurt feelings, disappointment, loneliness, or anger:** Guerrero, L. K., & La Valley, A. G. (2006). Conflict, emotion. The Sage handbook of conflict communication: Integrating theory, research, and practice, 69.

page 74 **the key to cultivating and maintaining quality bonds with our family is the ability to repair ruptures:** Gottman, J. M. (2011). The science of trust: Emotional attunement for couples. WW Norton & Company.

page 74 **Conflict followed by some kind of repair teaches children to problem solve and find solutions to nurture their relationships:** Jones, T. S. (2004). Conflict resolution education: The field, the findings, and the future. Conflict Resol. Q., 22, 233.

page 74 **the repair process gets initiated by someone making a bid for connection:** Gottman, J. M. (2008). Gottman method couple therapy. Clinical handbook of couple therapy, 4(8), 138-164.

page 74 **People who are able to successfully initiate and complete this repair process tend to have healthier and more stable relationships:** Meunier, V., & Baker, W. (2011). Positive couple relationships: The evidence for long-lasting relationship satisfaction and happiness. In Positive relationships: Evidence based practice across the world (pp. 73-89). Dordrecht: Springer Netherlands.

page 74 **becomes nearly impossible when dealing with family members who are emotionally immature:** Gibson, L. C. (2019). Recovering from Emotionally Immature Parents: Practical Tools to Establish Boundaries and Reclaim Your Emotional Autonomy. New Harbinger Publications.

page 74 **keeps the relationship in a state of discontent:** Grimmer, A. (2019). The cycle of rupture and repair in close relationships. Retrieved from https://www.bristolcbt.co.uk/publications/the-cycle-of-rupture-and-repair-in-close-relationships/

page 75 **Family over everything is a rule of behavior that individuals prefer to conform to on the condition that…:** Adapted from Bicchieri, C. (2006). The grammar of society: The nature and dynamics of social norms. Cambridge University Press.

page 75 **consistent, unresolved conflict with a family member can be costly and detrimental to one's mental health:** Gibson, L. C. (2019). Recovering from Emotionally Immature Parents: Practical Tools to Establish Boundaries and Reclaim Your Emotional Autonomy. New Harbinger Publications.

page 75 **One of the most drastic ways people cope with these difficult family members is through estrangement:** Agllias, K. (2018). Missing family: The adult child's experience of parental estrangement. Journal of Social Work Practice, 32(1), 59-72.

page 75 **boundary-setting is a necessary strategy:** Scharp, K. M., & Dorrance Hall, E. (2017). Family marginalization, alienation, and estrangement: Questioning the nonvoluntary status of family relationships. Annals of the International Communication Association, 41(1), 28-45.

page 76 **going no contact with a family member is not the norm:** Collins, L.M. (2022) How many Americans are estranged from family members? Retrieved from https://www.deseret.com/ 2022/12/21/23517721/1-in-4-americans-is-estranged-from-their-family-members/

page 76 **we also open ourselves up to criticism and even vilification from those who don't share this understanding:** Van Kleef, G. A., Wanders, F., Stamkou, E., & Homan, A. C. (2015). The social dynamics of breaking the rules: Antecedents and consequences of norm-violating behavior. Current Opinion in Psychology, 6, 25-31.

page 76 **should work to mend the relationship instead:** Scharp, K. M., Thomas, L. J., & Paxman, C. G. (2015). "It was the straw that broke the camel's back": Exploring the distancing processes communicatively constructed in parent–child estrangement backstories. Journal of Family Communication, 15, 330–348.

page 76 **Few openly discuss their experiences:** Scharp, K. M. (2016). Parent–child estrangement: Conditions for disclosure and perceived social network member reactions. Family Relations, 65, 688–700.

CHAPTER SEVEN: WEDDING BELLS

page 89 **"We loved with a love that was more than love":** Poe, E.A., 1809-1849. (1987). Annabel Lee: the Poem. Montréal: Tundra Books.

page 91 **Some believe it originated with the Egyptians:** Maskell, J. (1868). The Wedding-ring: Its History, Literature, and the Superstitions Respecting It. A Lecture, Etc. Simpkin, Marshall & Co.

page 91 **while others trace it back to the Romans:** Liliana, G. (2018). The Engagement. Evolution and Legal Effects. Studii Juridice şi Administrative, 18(1), 102-120.

page 91 **a ring was placed on the "ring finger" of the left hand:** Swinburne, H. (1686). A treatise of spousals, or matrimonial contracts wherein all the questions relating to that subject are ingeniously debated and resolved / by the late famous and learned Mr. Henry Swinburne, author of the Treatise of wills and testaments. S. Roycroft.

page 91 **but rather a sign of ownership:** Simmonds, A. (2024). Rings of power: a legal history of the engagement ring in early twentieth-century Australia. History Australia, 21(3), 398-415.

page 91 **woven reeds and leather:** Hersch, K. K. (2010). The Roman wedding: ritual and meaning in antiquity. Cambridge University Press.

page 92 **De Beers' "Diamonds are Forever" campaign:** Bergenstock, D. J., & Maskulka, J. M. (2001). The de beers story: are diamonds forever?. Business Horizons, 44(3), 37-44.

page 92 **making them a symbol of marriage and a societal expectation:** Bergenstock, D. J., & Maskulka, J. M. (2001). The de beers story: are diamonds forever?. Business Horizons, 44(3), 37-44.

page 92 **diamonds account for 85-90% of the engagement ring market:** The Dor Guide. (n.d.). Why Diamonds are still the number one choice for engagement rings. Retrieved from https://www. diamondsonrichmond.co.nz/essentials/dor-guide/why-diamonds-are-still-the-number-one-choice-for-engagement-rings#: ~:text=What%20percentage%20of%20engagement%20rings, feature%20at%20least%20one%20diamond.

page 92 **a typical wedding today in the U.S. costs about $35,000 with an average guest list of 115 people:** The Knot. (2024). The Knot 2023 Real Weddings Study. Retrieved from https://www.theknotww.com/ press-releases/wedding-guests-take-center-stage-the-knot-2023-real-weddings-study-reveals-75-of-couples-prioritize-the-guest-experience-when-planning-their-weddings/#: ~:text=Guest%20count%20was%20an%20average, up%20from%20%2430%2C000%20in%202022.

page 92 **In medieval times, the first documented wedding was a simple public announcement with a kiss:** Finnell, C. (2018). A history and analysis of weddings and wedding planning. Honors Theses-Providence Campus, 34(1), 1-61.

page 93 **Having a conventional wedding is a rule of behavior that individuals prefer to conform to on the condition that…:** Adapted from Bicchieri, C. (2006). The grammar of society: The nature and dynamics of social norms. Cambridge University Press.

page 94 **more than half of people describe the wedding planning process as "stressful":** Blomquist, L. (2024). How to Manage Wedding Planning Stress. Retrieved from https://www.brides.com/story/how-to-handle-wedding-planning-stress-zola-study

page 94 **recommends only spending 10% of your combined salary on your special day:** Financial Samurai. (2018). Who Should Pay For The Wedding? A Logical Guide To Lavish Spending. Retrieved from https:/ /www.financialsamurai.com/who-should-pay-for-the-wedding-follow-the-10-wedding-payment-rule/#: ~:text=1)%20Spend%20no%20more%20than, a%20median%20household%20income%20earner.

CHAPTER EIGHT: ZERO PROOF

page 107 **"Not drinking makes me a lot happier":** Campbell, N. (2013). Life & Style Interview. Retrieved from https://www.wmagazine.com/ gallery/chrissy-teigen-brad-pitt-sober-celebrities

page 109 **For many, drinking a few times a week is considered normal:** Boersma, P., Villarroel, M. A., & Vahratian, A. (2020). Heavy drinking among US adults, 2018. Retrieved from https://www.cdc. gov/nchs/products/databriefs/db374.htm

Page 109 **Alcohol has been around for thousands of years:** Phillips, R. (2014). Alcohol: A history. UNC Press Books.

page 109 **By the 1800s, it was already deeply ingrained in American culture, with widespread heavy drinking:** Blocker Jr, J. S. (2006). Did prohibition really work? Alcohol prohibition as a public health innovation. American Journal of Public Health, 96(2), 233-243.

page 109 **This sparked moral objections from prohibitionists:** Blocker Jr, J. S. (2006). Did prohibition really work? Alcohol prohibition as a public health innovation. American Journal of Public Health, 96(2), 233-243.

page 109 **In 1919, Prohibition—a nationwide alcohol ban—was officially passed by Congress in the U.S.:** Blocker Jr, J. S. (2006). Did prohibition really work? Alcohol prohibition as a public health innovation. American Journal of Public Health, 96(2), 233-243.

page 109 **it failed to stop people from drinking, ultimately leading to its repeal in 1933:** Blocker Jr, J. S. (2006). Did prohibition really work? Alcohol prohibition as a public health innovation. American Journal of Public Health, 96(2), 233-243.

page 109 **Today, about 63% of Americans drink alcohol, a figure that has remained stable since the Civil War:** Gallup. (2022). What percentage of Americans drink alcohol? Retrieved from https://news.gallup.com/poll/467507/percentage-americans-drink-alcohol.aspx

page 109 **reduced stress and improvements in physical and mental health:** Peele, S., & Brodsky, A. (2000). Exploring psychological benefits associated with moderate alcohol use: A necessary corrective to assessments of drinking outcomes? Drug and Alcohol Dependence, 60(3), 221-247.

page 109 **also feel more socially connected:** Sayette, M. A., Creswell, K. G., Dimoff, J. D., Fairbairn, C. E., Cohn, J. F., Heckman, B. W., ... & Moreland, R. L. (2012). Alcohol and group formation: A multimodal investigation of the effects of alcohol on emotion and social bonding. Psychological Science, 23(8), 869-878.

page 109 **The alcohol industry is notorious for downplaying the dangers while overemphasizing the benefits:** Petticrew, M., Maani Hessari, N., Knai, C., & Weiderpass, E. (2018). How alcohol industry organisations mislead the public about alcohol and cancer. Drug and Alcohol Review, 37(3), 293-303.

page 109 **alcohol is a leading cause of premature death and has been linked to cancer and various other illnesses:** Sohi, I., Franklin, A., Chrystoja, B., Wettlaufer, A., Rehm, J., & Shield, K. (2021). The global impact of alcohol consumption on premature mortality and health in 2016. Nutrients, 13(9), 3145.

page 109 **increase depression and anxiety:** Haynes, J. C., Farrell, M., Singleton, N., Meltzer, H., Araya, R., Lewis, G., & Wiles, N. J. (2005). Alcohol consumption as a risk factor for anxiety and depression: Results from the longitudinal follow-up of the National Psychiatric Morbidity Survey. The British Journal of Psychiatry, 187(6), 544-551.

page 110 **Drinking alcohol is a rule of behavior that individuals prefer to conform to on the condition that...:** Adapted from Bicchieri, C. (2006). The grammar of society: The nature and dynamics of social norms. Cambridge University Press.

page 110 **their friends can greatly influence their decisions about drinking**: Borsari, B., & Carey, K. B. (2001). Peer influences on college drinking: A review of the research. Journal of Substance Abuse, 13(4), 391-424.

page 110 **Peer pressure can be direct**: Kim, Y. M., & Neff, J. A. (2010). Direct and indirect effects of parental influence upon adolescent alcohol use: A structural equation modeling analysis. Journal of Child & Adolescent Substance Abuse, 19(3), 244-260.

page 110 **More subtle forms include**: Borsari, B., & Carey, K. B. (2001). Peer influences on college drinking: A review of the research. Journal of Substance Abuse, 13(4), 391-424.

page 110 **popular kids at school drink, it can create the illusion that "everyone" is doing it**: Borsari, B., & Carey, K. B. (2001). Peer influences on college drinking: A review of the research. Journal of Substance Abuse, 13(4), 391–424.

page 111 **many people develop strategies**: Morris, H., Larsen, J., Catterall, E., Moss, A. C., & Dombrowski, S. U. (2020). Peer pressure and alcohol consumption in adults living in the UK: A systematic qualitative review. BMC Public Health, 20, 1-13.

page 111 **Millennials and Gen Z are at the forefront of questioning alcohol's role in society**: Saad, L. (2023). Young adults in U.S. drinking less than in prior decades. Retrieved from https://news.gallup.com/poll/509690/young-adults-drinking-less-prior-decades.aspx

page 111 **many are choosing to drink less than previous generations**: Saad, L. (2023). Young adults in U.S. drinking less than in prior decades. Retrieved from https://news.gallup.com/poll/509690/young-adults-drinking-less-prior-decades.aspx

page 111 **Concerns about acting out of character and having those moments captured on social media**: Gerhold, J. (2019). New market, new rules: How Gen Z's are changing the alcohol industry. Retrieved from https://www.thinkwithgoogle.com/intl/en-emea/future-of-marketing/management-and-culture/diversity-and-inclusion/new-market-new-rules-how-genzs-are-changing-alcohol-industry/

page 111 **While some are reducing alcohol consumption in favor of other substances like cannabis and psychedelics**: National Institutes of Health. (2022). Marijuana and hallucinogen use among young adults reached all-time high in 2021. New Releases.

page 111 **the majority still drink:** Saad, L. (2023). Young adults in U.S. drinking less than in prior decades. Retrieved from https://news.gallup.com/poll/509690/young-adults-drinking-less-prior-decades.aspx

page 111 **predicts alcohol consumption may follow a path similar to tobacco use:** Whitaker, H. G. (2020). Quit like a woman: The radical choice to not drink in a culture obsessed with alcohol. Bloomsbury Publishing Plc.

CHAPTER NINE: AMERICAN DREAM

page 121 **"The American Dream is a phrase that we'll have to wrestle with all of our lives. It means a lot of things to different people. I think we're redefining it now":** Dove, R. (2019). Redefining the American Dream. Retrieved from https://blogs.vcu.edu/president/2019/07/03/redefining-the-american-dream/

page 123 **The idea was popularized by historian James Truslow Adams in 1931 during the Great Depression:** Wills, M. (2015). James Truslow Adams: Dreaming Up the American Dream. Retrieved from https://daily.jstor.org/james-truslow-adams-dreaming-american-dream/

page 123 **original ideals:** Beach, J. M. (2007). The ideology of the American dream: Two competing philosophies in education, 1776-2006. Educational studies, 41(2), 148-164.

page 123 **"dream of a better, richer, and happier life for all":** Wills, M. (2015). James Truslow Adams: Dreaming Up the American Dream. Retrieved from https://daily.jstor.org/james-truslow-adams-dreaming-american-dream/

page 123 **shifted from an inspiring message of solidarity and equality to one focused on consumerism:** Wills, M. (2015). James Truslow Adams: Dreaming Up the American Dream. Retrieved from https://daily.jstor.org/james-truslow-adams-dreaming-american-dream/

page 123 **Homeownership became a foundational element:** Bucchianeri, G. W. (2009). The American dream? The private and external benefits of homeownership. Work. Pap., Whart. Sch. Bus.

page 123 **In the 1950s, many people moved to the suburbs after the war to live "the good life":** Bourne, L. S. (1996). Reinventing the suburbs: Old myths and new realities. Progress in planning, 46(3), 163-184.

page 123 **the importance of homeownership was reinforced in society:** Quelch, J. (2008, October 27). How Marketing the American Dream Caused Our Economic Crisis. https://hbr.org/2008/10/the-current-economic-crisis-ha

page 123 **a rise in the American Dream being associated with consumer goods:** Ivanova, M. N. (2011). Consumerism and the crisis: wither 'the American dream'?. Critical Sociology, 37(3), 329-350.

page 123 **people started filling their homes with "more, new, and better" household items:** Shanken, A. M. (2006). Better Living: Toward a Cultural History of a Business Slogan. Enterprise & Society, 7(3), 485-519.

page 123 **People started buying the newest appliances and products, which caused many to feel pressure to conform and keep up with their neighbors:** Lavin, S. (2011). Scenes from the Suburbs. Journal of the Society of Architectural Historians, 70(3), 398-400.

page 124 **Education became an essential pathway to securing a good-paying job, which is considered the gateway to the American Dream:** Hochschild, J. L., & Scovronick, N. (2000). Democratic education and the American dream. Rediscovering the democratic purposes of education.

page 124 **Access to education is key to upward mobility for many:** Lin, M. L. (2020). Educational upward mobility. Practices of social changes-research on social mobility and educational inequality. Int'l J. Soc. Sci. Stud., 8, 25.

page 124 **In the 2000s, companies started adding degree requirements to job postings that didn't previously require degrees:** Fuller, J., Langer, C., Sigelman, M. (2022). Skills-Based Hiring is on the Rise. Retrieved from https://hbr.org/2022/02/skills-based-hiring-is-on-the-rise

page 124 **Chasing the American Dream is a rule of behavior that individuals prefer to conform to on the condition that...:** Adapted from Bicchieri, C. (2006). The grammar of society: The nature and dynamics of social norms. Cambridge University Press.

page 125 **Younger people are starting to forge a new path with an updated outlook on what the American Dream means:** Abel, N. (2023). New Poll Reveals Young Americans' Outlook on Future, Barriers to Success, and the American Dream. Retrieved from https://www.american.edu/media/news/20230914_newsineinstitutepollresults.cfm

page 125 **question the value of a college education that results in massive debt, favoring alternative avenues:** Burt, C. (2022). Why 50% of Gen Z students say they see less value in college degrees. Retrieved from https://universitybusiness.com/why-50-of-gen-z-students-say-they-see-less-value-in-college-degrees/

page 125 **There are significant barriers keeping them from homeownership:** Remax News. (2024). Nearly Two-Thirds of Gen Z and Millennials Are Ready to Become Homeowners, Prices Are Holding Them Back. Retrieved from https://news.remax.com/new-survey-finds-nearly-two-thirds-of-gen-z-and-millennials-are-ready-to-become-homeowners-whats-holding-them-back

page 125 **now have buyers' remorse:** Frishberg, H. (2024). Here's how many millennials regret their first home purchase. Retrieved from https://nypost.com/2024/01/23/real-estate/a-whopping-90-of-millennials-regret-buying-their-first-home/

page 125 **some are more interested in flexible mid-level jobs that allow more time to experience life:** Kato, B. (2023). Why Gen Z workers are rejecting 'hustle culture' — and what comes next. Retrieved from https://nypost.com/2023/10/07/snail-girl-how-gen-z-workers-are-ditching-hustle-culture-now/

page 125 **Younger generations aren't favoring just any life experiences; instead, they are prioritizing new ones:** Dublino, J. (2024). Experience Over Goods: The Millennial Shift in Spending. Retrieved from https://www.business.com/articles/experience-over-goods-the-millennial-shift-in-spending/

page 125 **Novel experiences are important because they grab our attention and slow time down, while monotony speeds time up:** Hammond, C. (2012). Time warped: Unlocking the mysteries of time perception. House of Anansi.

page 125 **thanks to a concept called the oddball effect:** Ulrich, R., & Bausenhart, K. M. (2019). The temporal oddball effect and related phenomena: Cognitive mechanisms and experimental approaches. The illusions of time: Philosophical and psychological essays on timing and time perception, 71-89.

page 125 **That's why young people are spending their money on travel:** Louis, S. (2023). Roughly 60% of millennials, Gen Z would rather spend money on 'life experiences' like traveling, concerts now than save for retirement — are they making a big mistake? Retrieved from https://finance.yahoo.com/news/roughly-60-millennials-gen-z-110000580.html

CHAPTER TEN: SMILE LINES

page 137 **"Your face is marked with lines of life, put there by love and laughter, suffering and tears. It's beautiful...":** Sands, L. (n.d.). Lynsay Sands. Retrieved from Goodreads.com

page 138 **this negative view of aging is deeply ingrained in American society:** M. Diehl, H.W. Wahl, A. Brothers, & M. Miche. (2015). Subjective aging and awareness of aging: Toward a new understanding of the aging self. Springer Publishing Company.

page 138 **Older adults are often stereotyped:** Dionigi, R. A. (2015). Stereotypes of aging: Their effects on the health of older adults. Journal of Geriatrics, 2015(1), 954027

page 138 **resulting in many being discriminated against as they age:** Voss, P., Bodner, E., & Rothermund, K. (2018). Ageism: The relationship between age stereotypes and age discrimination. Contemporary perspectives on ageism, 11-31.

page 139 **youth and beauty are glorified:** Jenull, B., Frate, N., & Mayer, C. (2018). Forever young? The desire for attractiveness and youthfulness at advanced age. US-China Foreign Language, 16, 487-501.

page 139 **Women aged 25 to 44 are most concerned about aging, but this anxiety is now affecting younger generations:** Bido, T. (2017). This Is the Generation MOST Worried About Aging. Retrieved from https://www.newbeauty.com/millennials-reportedly-worry-more-about-aging-than-their-moms-or-grandmothers/

page 139 **This desire for youthfulness fuels the multibillion-dollar beauty industry:** Petersen, A., & Seear, K. (2009). In search of immortality: The political economy of anti-aging medicine. Medicine Studies, 1(3), 267-279.

page 139 **The practice of hiding signs of aging dates back to 1500 BC when Egyptians used henna to conceal their gray hair:** de Groot, A. C. (2013). Side-effects of henna and semi-permanent 'black henna' tattoos: a full review. Contact dermatitis, 69(1), 1-25.

page 139 **Later, the Greeks and Romans used plant extracts to dye their hair as well:** Wisniak, J. (2004). Dyes from antiquity to synthesis. Indian journal of history of science, 39(1), 75-100.

page 139 **A few hundred years later, companies like L'Oréal and Clairol introduced more permanent dyes and the option to dye our hair at home:** Citron-Fink, R. (2019). True Roots: What Quitting Hair Dye Taught Me about Health and Beauty. Island Press.

page 139 **In the 1940s, only 7 percent of American women dyed their hair, but by the 1970s, that figure had grown to 40 percent:** Marshall, S. (2015). When, and Why, Did Women Start Dyeing Their Gray Hair? Retrieved from https://www.elle.com/beauty/hair/news/a30556/when-and-why-did-women-start-dyeing-their-gray-hair/

page 139 **In the 1980s, Clairol began marketing toward women's anxieties around aging, calling gray hair dull, drab, and "the ruination of romance":** Marshall, S. (2015). When, and Why, Did Women Start Dyeing Their Gray Hair? Retrieved from https://www.elle.com/beauty/hair/news/a30556/when-and-why-did-women-start-dyeing-their-gray-hair/

page 139 **Today, the majority of women dye their hair:** Marshall, S. (2015). When, and Why, Did Women Start Dyeing Their Gray Hair? Retrieved from https://www.elle.com/beauty/hair/news/a30556/when-and-why-did-women-start-dyeing-their-gray-hair/

page 139 **While most people aren't getting cosmetic work done:** Scianna, T. (2023). 24% of Americans Have Undergone a Cosmetic Treatment or Procedure: RealSelf Culture Report. Retrieved from https://www.medestheticsmag.com/news/news/22865217/24-of-americans-have-undergone-a-cosmetic-treatment-or-procedure-realself-culture-report

page 139 **the number of those who do has grown:** American Society of Plastic Surgeons. (2024). Plastic Surgery Sees Steady Growth Amidst Economic Uncertainty, American Society of Plastic Surgeons 2023 Procedural Statistics Report Finds. Retrieved from https://www.plasticsurgery.org/news/press-releases/plastic-surgery-sees-steady-growth-amidst-economic-uncertainty-american-society-of-plastic-surgeons-2023-procedural-statistics-report-finds

page 139 **the more time you spend on social media, the more likely you are to want to alter your appearance with cosmetic procedures:** Khan, I. F., De La Garza, H., Lazar, M., Kennedy, K. F., & Vashi, N. A. (2024). Effects of the COVID-19 Pandemic On Patient Social Media Use and Acceptance of Cosmetic Procedures. The Journal of Clinical and Aesthetic Dermatology, 17(3), 42.

page 140 **Being anti-aging is a rule of behavior that individuals prefer to conform to on the condition that…:** Adapted from Bicchieri, C. (2006). The grammar of society: The nature and dynamics of social norms. Cambridge University Press.

page 140 **Increased confidence can have a positive ripple effect on our relationships, careers, and overall happiness:** Ribeiro, F., & Steiner, D. (2018). Quality of life before and after cosmetic procedures on the face: A cross-sectional study in a public service. Journal of Cosmetic Dermatology, 17(5), 688-692.

page 140 **shifting our mindset about aging can help us be happier and live longer:** Levy, B. R., Slade, M. D., Kunkel, S. R., & Kasl, S. V. (2002). Longevity increased by positive self-perceptions of aging. Journal of personality and social psychology, 83(2), 261.

page 141 **The media often reinforces stereotypes about aging:** Raina, D., & Balodi, G. (2014). Ageism and stereotyping of the older adults. Scholars Journal of Applied Medical Sciences, 2(2C), 733-739.

page 141 **organizations such as Hollywood, Health & Society (HHS) is working to ensure realistic depictions of aging in shows and movies:** Sloane, J. (2023). Aging on Screen and on the Page: Changing Depictions of Older People in the Media. Retrieved from https://www. asc.upenn.edu/news-events/news/aging-screen-and-page-changing-depictions-older-people-media

page 141 **can help lessen anxiety around aging:** Davis, E. C., & Graf, A. S. (2024). Intergenerational Contact in Young Adults in Relation to Aging Anxiety, Attitudes, and Future Time Perspective. Journal of Intergenerational Relationships, 22(1), 56-72.

page 141 **Encouraging intergenerational relationships can also foster a more positive view of aging:** Davis, E. C., & Graf, A. S. (2024). Intergenerational Contact in Young Adults in Relation to Aging Anxiety, Attitudes, and Future Time Perspective. Journal of Intergenerational Relationships, 22(1), 56-72.

page 141 **Policies that promote intergenerational connections like combining nurseries, youth clubs, and nursing homes:** Butts, D.M., & Jarrott, S.E. (2021). The Power of Proximity: Co-Locating Childcare and Eldercare Programs. Retrieved from https://ssir.org/articles/entry/ the_power_of_proximity_co_locating_childcare_and_eldercare_ programs

CHAPTER ELEVEN: BEYOND THE IMAGINABLE

page 154 **People are happiest when their time is spent doing things they want to do rather than things they feel obligated to do:** Hofer, J., & Busch, H. (2012). Living in accordance with one's implicit motives: cross-cultural evidence for beneficial effects of motive-goal congruence and motive satisfaction. In A positive psychology perspective on quality of life (pp. 51-66). Dordrecht: Springer Netherlands.